**Secrets of the Duke's Family**

*The mysteries and passions of the aristocracy!*

Lady Margaret and Lady Olivia are hoping
their brother, the Duke of Scofield, will sponsor
a season for them. They're desperate to start their
lives and to find the fairy-tale romance that
awaits them in society's ballrooms.

But with rumors circulating that the duke murdered
their father to get the title, scandal stalks the
family wherever they turn. They must weather the
storm as the truth is revealed...and as they fall,
unexpectedly, irresistibly in love along the way!

Read Margaret's story in:
*Lady Margaret's Mystery Gentleman*

Read Olivia's story in:
*Lady Olivia's Forbidden Protector*

You won't want to miss
the last book in Christine Merrill's
Secrets of the Duke's Family trilogy

Coming soon!

## Author Note

In this book, I had a chance to send my heroine, Lady Olivia, to Vauxhall Gardens in disguise. To hide her identity, she tells her maid to find her a domino and a mask.

Nowadays, we tend to think of a domino and a mask as being the same thing. The word *domino* has come to describe the little half mask that covers the nose and has two eyeholes like the spots on a domino tile.

But in the Regency era, a domino referred to the robe worn with a mask. It was an ample robe with wide sleeves and possibly capelets and a hood. A lady could hide even a large gown under a domino, and with the addition of a mask, she'd be completely unrecognizable.

Happy reading.

# CHRISTINE MERRILL

---

## Lady Olivia's Forbidden Protector

**HARLEQUIN®**
# HISTORICAL™

ISBN-13: 978-1-335-40731-3

Lady Olivia's Forbidden Protector

This edition published by arrangement with Harlequin Books S.A.

For questions and comments about the quality of this book, please contact us at CustomerService@Harlequin.com.

Harlequin Enterprises ULC
22 Adelaide St. West, 40th Floor
Toronto, Ontario M5H 4E3, Canada
www.Harlequin.com

**Printed in U.S.A.**

**Christine Merrill** lives on a farm in Wisconsin with her husband, two sons and too many pets—all of whom would like her to get off the computer so they can check their email. She has worked by turns in theater costuming and as a librarian. Writing historical romance combines her love of good stories and fancy dress with her ability to stare out the window and make stuff up.

### Books by Christine Merrill

### Harlequin Historical

*The Brooding Duke of Danforth*
*Snowbound Surrender*
*"Their Mistletoe Reunion"*
*Vows to Save Her Reputation*

### Secrets of the Duke's Family

*Lady Margaret's Mystery Gentleman*
*Lady Olivia's Forbidden Protector*

### Those Scandalous Stricklands

*Regency Christmas Wishes*
*"Her Christmas Temptation"*
*A Kiss Away from Scandal*
*How Not to Marry an Earl*

### The Society of Wicked Gentlemen

*A Convenient Bride for the Soldier*

### The de Bryun Sisters

*The Truth About Lady Felkirk*
*A Ring from a Marquess*

Visit the Author Profile page
at Harlequin.com for more titles.

To all of us.
It's been a long two years.

# Chapter One

Michael Solomon came down the stairs to breakfast in his house on Gracechurch Street, thoroughly satisfied with the fineness of the morning and life in general. It was often thus at the beginning of a new assignment, when he was still confident in the ease of the task put to him. He would likely feel different by supper tomorrow, after a full day of dealing with the nobility and their foolishness. But at least for the moment all was well.

He kissed the woman waiting for him at the table, feeling equally magnanimous towards her. 'Good morning, Mother.'

She beamed at him, pouring out his coffee before he asked for it. 'Did you sleep well, my dear?'

'Excellently, thank you,' he said, smiling back at her and heaping his plate with eggs and ham.

She nodded in approval. 'It is always best to start a job well rested and fully nourished.' Then she steepled her fingers and leaned forward eagerly. 'What is it to be this time? Chasing jewel thieves? Thwarting black-mailers? Intercepting French contraband?'

He shook his head, partly in denial and partly in frustration. His mother never seemed to understand that enquiry agents were hired for their discretion and were not supposed to share the details of their employers' business with all and sundry. 'Nothing so exciting as you imagine. I am to be a bodyguard for an heiress.' His description made the job sound far more interesting than it was likely to be. The risks to the girl were minimal, other than those she created for herself.

'Is she very pretty?' his mother asked, eyebrows raised.

'I do not know,' he said. 'I have not met her as yet.' Most likely, she was. In his experience, enough money and sufficient rank could make even the plainest girl seem handsome. It hardly mattered one way or another. It was not his job to have an opinion on such things, nor was he the sort to covet women he could not have.

'And why does she need a bodyguard?' Her eyes widened. 'Is it kidnappers?'

He sighed. 'She has formed an inappropriate liaison, and I am to prevent the elopement.'

His mother seemed to deflate, disappointed. 'Why would you do such a horrible thing as to stand in the way of young love?'

'Someone must,' he said, silently amazed that she, of all people, would not see the reason for it.

'For all you know, it is her only chance at happiness. At the very least, it is terribly romantic.'

'Far from it,' he countered. 'I would call it foolish. She is the sister of a duke. It is up to her brother to decide who she will marry. If he does not like this fellow, then he cannot be worthy of her.'

'The sister of a duke,' she said, snatching at a piece of information he had not meant to reveal. She put a finger to her chin. 'Now let me see. Who has a sister of marriageable age? Exeter? Norfolk?'

'You know I do not like to discuss the identity of my clients,' he said, trying to focus on his breakfast, as if it might halt her speculation.

'Folbroke is an only child. Felkirk has a brother.'

'You should be the enquiry agent, rather than I,' he said. 'You ask questions enough to be one.' Then he took a large bite of toast to make an answer impossible.

'Do not say it is Scofield,' she said, watching him carefully and searching for a reaction. 'It is, isn't it? Oh, dear.'

He waved his napkin in surrender and continued to chew.

'I do not need words to get the truth out of you,' she said, taking his silence for assent. 'You should not work for such a man. It is common knowledge that he is a murderer. He stabbed his father to death, then took his title and his seat in Parliament without even a day of mourning.'

'Just because everyone knows a story does not make

it true,' he said. From what he had learned before taking this assignment, this was the exception to that rule. There had been a murder, and the new Scofield had likely killed the older. He had worn black at the funeral, but few had given him credit for it, since he had not seemed the least bit sorry at his father's passing.

But a lack of tears was not enough evidence for a conviction, and it was not Michael's job to speculate. 'There is no reason for you to be concerned on my account. When I met the man, he did not seem any more murderous or mad than the other peers I have met. And he is not likely to kill me since he has nothing to gain from doing so.'

He had meant to make light of the situation, but the humour was lost on his mother, who clucked her tongue in disapproval.

'He wishes you to thwart the love of his sister, who only wants to get away from him,' she said, shaking her head, obviously disappointed in him.

'More likely, he has some other, more appropriate man in mind,' Michael said, trying to be reasonable. 'It is his duty as her guardian to keep her from marrying the wrong man.'

'And I assume you have investigated the fellow she wants to run off with,' his mother said, eyes narrowed. 'What is the trouble with him?'

'None that I can see,' Michael said with a shrug. 'He seems unexceptionable. But as long as the Duke is paying me, it is not up to me to judge the man. It is merely my job to carry out his commands. If he wishes Alister Clement to have no contact with his sister, Lady Olivia, so shall it be.'

'And I suppose there was no mention of the other sister,' she said, frowning. 'The gossip sheets say there has been no sign of her for some months. Given Scofield's reputation...'

'There is nothing particularly ominous about it,' Michael said as he reached for the toast rack. 'It was another elopement. Scofield probably regrets that he did not hire me earlier. And you should not waste your time obsessing on the affairs of the *ton*,' he added, knowing it was pointless to tell her so. They were both far removed from that part of society and he could not understand her fascination with the comings and goings of people she would never meet.

His mother sighed, then said, 'Your father and I eloped.'

'I am aware of that,' he said.

'It was quite the scandal at the time.'

He did not reply, trying to concentrate on his breakfast.

'Mr Solomon, God bless his soul, used to say to me...'

'Please,' Michael said, pinching the bridge of his nose and closing his eyes against the story likely to follow. 'May we not have any discussion of that man's opinions? Since I never met him, his words of wisdom have been useless to me.'

His mother sighed again. It was a watery sound designed to make him regret his lapse in patience. 'His words were all that were left to give to you. It is not as if there was an inheritance to offer. When we married, his family cut him off without a penny.'

'Of course, they did,' Michael said with his own sigh, which was dry as dust. It was good that at least one of the people at the breakfast table had sense and skills enough to provide for them, since the phantom of John Solomon had been no use at all.

'When he disappeared, I was quite at a loss as to how to proceed,' she said with yet another sigh, tugging a handkerchief out of her sleeve and dabbing at her eyes.

'So you have told me,' Michael said, not adding *a thousand times*, merely thinking it. 'But it has been twenty-nine years or more.'

'And yet my time with him is as fresh to me as if it happened yesterday.'

'Of course,' Michael said, methodically chewing and swallowing to prevent him from speaking his mind. If the loss was as fresh as she claimed, she would not change the story each time she told it to him. Nor would she have quite so many words of wisdom from a man who had been with her a year at most. Through his childhood and manhood, she had told him so many tales of his father that she might have lived a lifetime with the fellow.

He had realised the brutal truth long before he was old enough to shave. His mother had a penchant for fiction and used it against him in the hope that he would form some attachment to a paragon that did not exist so he would not ache over the lack of a father.

Some men thrived because of their parentage, but he had done so in spite of it. Realising that he was alone and unwanted by his father had been the spur that goaded him to become the man he wanted to be. He took extra pride in his own achievements, knowing they had come from his own hand. Though his mother might still need a crutch, he had little use for fairy tales nor any use at all for Mr John Solomon.

Then she smiled. 'You and Lady Olivia will have something in common, being fatherless as you are.'

'Of course,' he said through gritted teeth. No matter how he wished to lash out at his mother, he contained himself. She had given every last bit of herself to keep him and deserved nothing but gratitude in return. But of all the nonsense she had prattled in his life, this was probably the furthest from the truth. No matter what she might think, there would not be an inch of common ground between the daughter of a deceased duke and an unacknowledged bastard.

Lady Olivia Bethune's hand tightened on the handle of the last basket as her brother's carriage pulled to a stop in front of an unfashionable house in an equally unfashionable neighbourhood.

Across from her, her maid Molly awakened with a

snort, lurching upward, and tried to pretend that she had not been sleeping between stops.

Liv held up a reassuring hand and gave her a sympathetic smile. 'It has been a long day for both of us. You needn't come in with me this time if you do not wish.'

'But His Grace says...' the maid began.

'What my brother does not know will not hurt him,' Liv assured her. 'And even he would not make a complaint at my visiting Mrs Wilson without a chaperone. She is past eighty and near deaf. What harm could she possibly do me?'

The maid nodded in agreement and gave her a proud smile. 'It is most kind of you to bring a basket of dainties to her and the other widows, my lady. My sister is in service at the Earl of Enderland's house, and her lady is not near so generous and thoughtful as you are to those less fortunate.'

Liv smiled back to hide the twinge of guilt tightening her throat. 'It is what my brother wishes for me, I am sure. If he means to keep me a spinster, I had best get used to a life of good works.'

She had spoken too honestly, for Molly looked back at her with a worried frown. 'But you do not look on it as a burden, I am sure. You are ever so much happier after the weekly visits you make.'

'Of course,' Liv said, relieved. 'It does me good to know that my ladies are happy. And I mean to see that they continue to get their baskets, even when I am gone.'

'Gone?' the maid said, surprised.

Liv forced a laugh to hide yet another misstep. 'Back to the country, of course. We cannot stay in London all year and I do not wish to leave disappointment in my wake.'

'Ahh,' Molly said, relieved.

'Nor do I want you to be overtaxed, fetching and carrying these hampers for me,' she said, smiling at the maid again. 'I can handle this one myself. I will have a nice chat with Mrs Wilson, and then we shall go home.' Before Molly could object again, she was out through the door that the coachman opened for her and halfway up the stairs to the widow's tiny flat. Once at the door, she rapped smartly on the panel, well aware that no amount of pounding would bring the deaf old woman to let her in.

It swung open almost before she was done and she was pulled quickly inside, the door shutting and locking behind her. 'I had begun to think that you would not come.' Alister Clement was waiting for her, just as he did each week when she made the last stop on her charitable visits. Now, he pulled her close for a brief kiss, which was interrupted by the cleared throat of the old woman in the corner.

'I will have no slap and tickle in my parlour,' Mrs Wilson said, shaking an already shaky finger. 'I will not stand for nonsense.'

'Of course not, Mrs Wilson,' Liv said in a loud voice, stepping away from Alister to prove her respectability. 'We would not dream of imposing after you have been so kind as to chaperone our meetings.' Then she pressed the basket she carried into the woman's hands. 'And here we have some calf's-foot jelly, a loaf of bread and a very nice cheese for you. Also, a bag of the boiled sweets you like so well.' She did not mention the bundle of coins tucked into the cloth that wrapped the Stilton. It seemed rude to acknowledge the extra bribe included for the lady's silence.

And silent she was, gathering the basket to her chest without another word and thrusting her withered hand into the bag of sweets. As Liv turned back to her beloved, the air filled with the scent of cloves and the sounds of industrious sucking.

'It has seemed like for ever,' she said, taking Alister's hand and letting him lead her to a sofa that was out of line with the view from the windows.

'Only a week,' he reminded her. 'Not as often as we were seeing each other when your brother was focused on containing your sister Margaret. But there is nothing to be done about that.'

In Liv's opinion, there was definitely something that could be done, but it was not her place to suggest it. Though Alister had been courting her for over two years, at times they seemed no closer to marriage than they had on the first day they'd met. To plan her own elopement seemed both unladylike and ungrateful of the attention he had given her, so she said nothing. Instead, she made sure that her expression was overbrimming with a proper amount of devotion and hinted for all she was worth. 'I miss you terribly when I cannot see you every day. With Peg gone and only my brother for company, it is very lonely.'

Alister nodded sympathetically and cast a glance in Mrs Wilson's direction before gathering her hand to his lips for a brief kiss. 'I understand completely. And now that Peg is finally out of the way, I see no reason for us to delay our future any longer.'

'Finally?' she said, her loving smile slipping for a moment.

'Well,' Alister said, adding a sound somewhere between a laugh and a huff of disapproval. 'Though one can hardly condone her unfortunate choice in husband, it is a relief to see her settled somewhere.'

Liv managed a response in a voice that was ever so slightly tight at the edges. 'She does not think it unfortunate, I am sure. My brother allows me no contact with her, since he thinks she will be a bad influence on me, but from what little he has let slip about her, she and Mr Castell are quite happily married.'

'And I suspect he is still a newspaper reporter,' Alister replied, his voice equally tight. 'Not the best connection she could have made, and it does your family no credit. But if she is happy, then that is something, I suppose.' He wrinkled his nose as if her sister's joy had the stench of the unwashed lower classes.

'She is much better off than she was when living under Hugh's thumb,' Liv insisted. 'It was intolerable.'

'Then she will not be tempted to return to Scofield

House with her tail between her legs, seeking forgiveness,' he said with a smile. 'And since Hugh has banned her from associating with you, we will not have to worry about her washing up on our doorstep once we have married.'

She blinked for a moment as the image of her sister, bedraggled and in need, knocked on imaginary doors, only to be turned away by both brother and sister. Then she brightened. 'I will not be bound by my brother's rules once I am your wife.' She disentangled her hand from his and walked her fingers up the front of his waistcoat. 'Surely you will not begrudge me a visit from my sister and new brother, should they be in the vicinity of our home.'

There was a pause before he answered, almost as if that had been exactly his intention. But apparently he did not want to spoil the mood any more than she did, and eventually he replied, 'Of course not.'

'That is good,' she said with a smile, relieved to have won this small argument about a thing that might never occur if Alister could not manage to come up to scratch and wed her.

'And it is not as if she would be coming to live with us,' he said, unable to keep the relief from his own voice. 'I know you feared that might be necessary when she was still at home and your brother would not allow her a season.'

'I did not precisely fear it…' she allowed. In fact, she had been looking forward to it. She had assumed that they would be inviting her sister into their home, once she and Alister had wed. Of course, since she was oldest, she had also assumed that her marriage would have happened long before Peg found a husband. She had been wrong in that as well.

Whenever she and Alister had discussed it before, something had always stood in the way of an elopement. Either the weather was wrong for a trip to Scotland, or Alister had some business that he could not manage to leave, even for a week's journey. And if not those reasons, then perhaps her brother was in a mood and watching too closely for her to get away. But, talking to him now, it seemed that there might be another, unspoken reason that had trumped them all.

'Well, it is good that we no longer have to care about housing Margaret,' Alister said with a smile, relaxing against the seat they shared and allowing his arm to drape behind her in a way that was almost an embrace.

Without intending to, she leaned forward, away from his arm, then turned to look at him in surprise. 'Would it really have bothered you so much to have her stay with us?'

The answer was preceded by another unfortunate delay, as if he had realised his misstep and was searching his mind for a way to minimise it. 'Of course not. But it is never ideal to have a guest in the house at the start of a marriage. I would not want you to have been distracted by her.'

Liv wanted to argue that there was nothing distracting about her sister, and that she was family and not a guest. But it seemed foolish to pick another fight over a point that had been rendered moot by Peg's elopement.

When she said nothing, Alister chose to take her silence for agreement. His hand closed on her shoulder, pulling her gently back to lean against his arm. 'Now that the matter is settled, we can begin to plan for our future.'

She rested uneasily against him, for until today she had not really known that there had been a hindrance to such plans. Apparently, he had been waiting until such time as he was sure that Peg was gone before proceeding. In some ways, this seemed an insult to her beloved sister.

But it might have been worse. He might have spirited her away to Scotland before telling her of his aversion to housing and launching Peg. Then, the poor thing would have been left to manage their brother on her own. Hugh being what he was, it would have been disastrous. Instead, the reverse was true. Peg was gone, and Liv was the one who was trapped. But her escape was finally imminent.

She smiled at Alister, reminding herself that it should be easy to forgive him for a thing that had not actually happened, and nodded in agreement. 'As you say, it has all worked out for the best. If you have plans, I am eager to hear of them.'

He started to speak and then glanced at the old lady in the corner, who was starting on another piece of candy. She showed no signs of having heard anything that they had said thus far, nor did she seem to care what might come next. Then he turned back to Liv, giving her hand a squeeze. 'Next week, come to see me here, as you always do. But include an extra hamper in your stack of gifts. Fill it with a change of linen, and any personal possessions you cannot do without. We will leave by the back stairs of this building, take a hired carriage to Scotland and be married in one week's time.'

One more week.

It was so soon. But she must remember that he had been waiting years for her, ignoring the refusal and scorn of both her father and brother. He had stood with her through the period of mourning, while ignoring the foul rumours about her brother's part in the death. Now that he was ready, it was unfair of her to keep him waiting a moment longer.

She smiled again and squeezed his hand in return. 'Until next week.'

He nodded, satisfied, and gave her a chaste kiss on the cheek. 'And now you must return to the carriage before the maid wonders at the delay. We will see each other again soon.' The look he was giving her now was different from the ones he had given her before, full of a warmth that was exciting and, if she was honest, a little frightening.

She took a deep breath to steady her nerves. 'The sooner the better.'

# Chapter Two

Six days.

After waiting for so long, it was strangely numbing to be so close to marriage. She had expected it to feel quite different from this. An impending elopement was supposed to be exciting. She had expected that she would find it difficult to sleep because her mind would be clouded with happy fantasies.

Instead, she had fallen into a fitful doze and woken sweat-soaked and with a scream on her lips. She had not expected the dreams to come back after all this time. They had plagued her almost nightly for months after the murder had occurred. It had been over two years since then, and lately they had been coming only once or twice a month.

But, now that she was alone in the house with Hugh, they were increasing again, and she woke almost daily with the memory of finding her father slumped over his desk as fresh in her mind as if it had happened yesterday.

To recover from the dream, she had lain in her bed listening to the longcase clock chiming off hours in the hall like a condemned man feeling his life slip away. It was a temporary disturbance of the mind, nothing more. Once she was on her way to Scotland and a new life, she was sure she would feel better. She would be out of this house and could leave behind the memories of the things she'd seen here, dropping them on the doorstep like so much unwanted baggage.

She could barely tolerate her current circumstances. She was near to being a prisoner in her brother's home. The doors were guarded against unapproved visitors, and she could not leave for any reason without being followed by servants and chaperoned by her maid.

Since their father's murder, Hugh had been obsessed with controlling both his sisters, refusing to allow them to go about in society like normal girls their age. He had denied them seasons, refused all suitors and even turned down invitations to routs and dinners, keeping them apart from friends and strangers alike. His constrictions had caused Peg to run away with the first man who offered. It was driving Liv away as well, if only so she might be free of the memories of her father.

Life away from Scofield House would have many advantages. As a married woman, she would have more freedom. Alister would not think twice about her going shopping or visiting friends. Once she was Mrs Clement and not just the sister of Scofield, there might be invitations to dinners and parties. If she could separate

herself from her notorious brother, society would have
no reason to gawp at her. Any stigma attached to her
reputation would dissipate. She could have a normal life.

The idea made her feel better immediately. Before
Father had died and Hugh had taken control of her and
her sister's futures, life had been quite ordinary. She'd
had a season, or most of one, at least. She'd danced and
flirted and been courted by several gentlemen. And then
the murder had happened, and everything had changed.

For a moment, everything seemed to freeze inside
her and the present was blotted out by another memory
of that night: the screaming, the blood and the feel of
Hugh's hands on her arms, trying to shake the panic
out of her as he dragged her from the study and away
from their father...

She took a deep breath, and then another, forcing the
vision out of her mind, focusing on the garden outside,
the leaves fluttering in the trees and the carefully tended
flowers banked at their roots. In less than a week, she
would be able to put the past behind her and have the
life she'd always hoped for. She stared at the gate at the
back of the garden and imagined the liberating feeling
of walking through it for the last time, never to return.

Then she started, surprised. There was a strange
gentleman on the bench under the laurel at the centre
of the garden. He was sitting so still that she had over-
looked him on the first scan of the space, but now she
focused on him, fascinated. He was reading, or at least
pretending to. His hat was tipped low over his eyes, ei-

ther to shade them from the sun or to hide the fact that he was napping. His legs were spread wide, one ankle perched on the opposite knee, in something more like a sprawl than a politely seated position.

She stared at him for a time, wondering at the audacity of it. It would have been bad enough if this stranger was treating their back garden like a public park. Instead, he acted as if it was his own property where he could do as he wished. She was not even sure how he had come to be there, since Hugh had set someone to watch the back gate to prevent her from sneaking through it. What good were the guards if they did not bother to stop strangers from getting in?

He did not appear to be a vagrant. Despite his lack of manners, he was clean and well dressed. The hair that was visible under his hat was properly trimmed, and the sort of golden blond that caused girls to sigh when it caught the candlelight at dinner. Though she could not see them, she suspected he had equally riveting blue eyes. The chin under the brim of the hat was strong, just the sort of stalwart English jaw that women couldn't resist.

She clenched her own jaw in response, refusing to be moved. Then she made her way through the kitchen to the garden door to investigate.

Once outside, she stopped at the kennel where her dogs were kept. At the sight of her, the older pug, Caesar, waddled forward and huffed a greeting.

'You are supposed to bark when there are intruders

present,' she said, pointing at the man and staring down at the dog in disapproval.

At one time, he would have growled at her in response. Caesar had been a contrary beast for most of his life. Today, he grinned back at her and wagged his tail.

She sighed as his mate, Cleopatra, scampered up to stand shoulder to shoulder with him, equally happy to see her and just as oblivious to the intruder.

Against her better judgement, she bent down and scratched their ears. 'Love makes fools of us all, Caesar. You have been quite useless since Cleo arrived. But at least you are happy, and I must take some pleasure in it.'

She gave him a final pat, then proceeded down the garden to confront the man sleeping on the bench. When he did not look up as she approached, she cleared her throat. When this elicited no response, she nudged his boot with the toe of her slipper and said in a loud voice, 'Excuse me.'

Showing no sign of alarm, he pushed his hat back on his head with the tip of one finger and stared up at her, his eyes clear of the fog of slumber.

Without meaning to, her breath caught in her throat. Those eyes were as blue as she'd assumed they'd be. The slow smile he displayed at the sight of her was equally distracting. 'Did you want something?' he said in a tone that implied she was the one disturbing him.

'Did *I* want something?' she repeated, astounded at the gall of the man.

He nodded. 'I assume you must. You are here and speaking to me, after all.'

'This is a private garden,' she said.

'I am aware of that,' he replied. 'I certainly would not nap in a public park.'

'It is my private garden,' she replied. 'My brother's, actually. The Duke of Scofield.'

The man on the bench nodded. 'I am aware of that as well.'

'He would be most unhappy to find you here,' she said, glancing towards the gate.

'He would be most unhappy to find me anywhere else,' the man said. 'Since he employs me to watch you, I could not think of a better place to do it.'

'You are working for my brother?' she said, now thoroughly surprised. 'You look nothing like the men he usually hires.' Hugh's typical guards were hulking brutes, more akin to carthorses than the thoroughbred occupying the bench in front of her.

'I was told that the previous men were not very good at their jobs,' he said with a shrug. 'Apparently, he decided to employ brains rather than brawn.'

'Of all the… Apparently, you are as vain as you are…' She stopped, for she was about to announce that she thought him handsome. His looks or those of the previous men should not have mattered at all. 'If you are working for my brother, you should not be lounging about in the garden.'

'I am working for your brother,' he agreed. 'But that

does not mean I will be taking orders from you.' Then he added, 'It was clear to me that you were not going anywhere. I could see you through the window, my lady. It is not necessary for me to march back and forth behind the house to prevent something that is not happening.'

The men who had watched her before had gone silently about their duties, ever present but never daring to speak to her or her sister. But this man was beyond insolent, calling her a lady while trampling over the social barriers between them as if they did not exist.

His behaviour was infuriating, but at least he was interesting. If he managed to get sacked on his first day, Lord knew who her brother might hire instead.

'Suppose I had left,' she said in a more reasonable tone. 'I might have walked right by you as you slept.'

'Without saying hello?' he said with mock surprise. 'That would have been most rude of you. Since I know you are a proper young lady, I expected you would stop to speak to me before leaving.'

That was not what a proper lady would do, and he was well aware of it. He was a stranger to her and, worse yet, an underling. Manners did not require her to acknowledge him at all.

'We have not been introduced,' she reminded him, hoping to put him in his place.

'I am Mr Michael Solomon.' He gave the faintest emphasis to the word Mr as if it pleased him to remind

her that a nobody had power over her comings and goings. Then he held out his hand to her.

She ignored it, staring at him in offended silence.

'And you are Lady Olivia Bethune,' he said, paying
no attention to the snub. 'You may call me Michael if
you wish. I suspect we will see a lot of each other in
the coming weeks. There is no reason to stand on ceremony.'

There was every need. She could not go around calling strange men by their first names, even if they were
little better than servants. And even a small intimacy
with a man who looked like Michael Solomon felt dangerous in a way she could not explain.

'I never bother to learn the names of the men my
brother sets to guard me,' she said, hoping to put him
in his place.

He smiled. 'Probably because they never bothered
to introduce themselves. I am happy to be the first.'

'But...'

He held up a hand as though he were fending off
compliments rather than preventing further censure. 'I
am sure we will get on much better than you did with
the previous men who have done this job.' His smile
widened. 'We are off to an excellent start. You have
come to talk to me on the very first day.'

'I do not normally see a reason to converse with my
jailers,' she snapped before he could deliberately misunderstand her again. Of course, the other guards had
been large, rough-looking men and, if she was honest,

they had quite frightened her. But there was something about Mr Solomon that frightened her in a far different way. She took a breath and tried to remember her place in society, and in this conversation. 'If I had spoken to them, I would have told them that they should not be sleeping in the garden when they were supposed to be working.'

'Would you rather that I came in the house and sat with you? Your brother might think it was improper. But if you prefer it...' His expression was innocent to the point of earnestness, but there was a glint in his eyes that said he knew how totally ridiculous the suggestion was and had only said it to torment her.

'I would prefer that you just go away,' she said, exasperated. 'I take no pleasure in being confined in my own home. I have done nothing to deserve such punishment.' He was new to the household. Lord knew what Hugh had told him about her. Perhaps it was still possible to make him understand. 'You may think that you have been brought here to prevent an unfortunate marriage. But, in truth, it does not matter who I might form an attachment to. My brother means to keep me a spinster for no logical reason and denies me contact with society or anyone who might help me escape him.'

At this, Mr Solomon shrugged, and all insolence disappeared. He became the loyal servant she should have known he was. 'If he is your guardian, that is for him to decide.'

'But you do not have to take part in the injustice,'

she replied. 'If you were a decent man, you would not take a job such as this.'

He shrugged again. 'If I were a man of independent means, like the men in your family, I would not have to work at all. But it might surprise you to learn that the majority of the people in England cannot afford to be particular when employment is offered to them, especially when it is something as sensible as preventing a wilful young lady from doing herself harm.'

She could not help a small gasp of shock. He might smile at her as if he were a gentleman talking to a lady, but he was not of her class. And there was an underlying bitterness in his words that announced her rank would earn her no sympathy with him. 'Your need of employment does not make my brother's treatment of me any more just,' she said, knowing that right and wrong did not matter to a man with bills to pay. 'As I said before, I have done nothing to deserve this confinement.'

'And as I have said before, it is no concern of mine.' He sighed in frustration, but his smile, which now seemed cold and professional, did not waver.

'This is why I did not bother to speak to the men who guarded me before,' she said, giving him a mocking imitation of his smile. 'There is no mercy to be had from someone who has been bought and paid for by a murderer. But, as you say, that is no concern of yours. I suppose I should be content with my lot. If he wanted *me* dead, I'd be gone by now.' She gave him a thoughtful look. 'You, however? I hope for your sake that he does nothing more serious than sack you, should I manage to escape.'

Then, before he could frame a retort, she turned on her heel and went back to the house.

Michael let out a slow breath as he watched Lady Olivia Bethune walking away from him. Stalking would be a more accurate description of her gait, but proper ladies did not stomp their feet, no matter how angry one made them. He had enraged her by playing the fool and it had given him great pleasure to do so.

It had offended her that he could sit comfortably in her garden while doing the job he had been hired for. She was probably the sort that reminded her servants of their place by forcing them to look busy, even if there was nothing to do. If he had not provoked her by his actions, she would not have spoken to him at all. She had all but admitted that her previous guards were far beneath her notice.

That made her parting words confusing. They had sounded like a warning to beware of her brother. It seemed she believed him a murderer, just as the rest of London did. If his own sister did not trust him, it confirmed the truth of the story, for who would know better than a member of the family?

In the brief interview he'd had with the Duke, Scofield had seemed cold-blooded but not homicidal. Michael had worked for murderers before, and they'd gone out of their way to appear innocent. But Scofield behaved as most peers did, as if it did not matter one way or another what people thought of him.

Nor had he shown any obvious signs of insanity. This was some comfort, at least. Though Michael had worked for mad men before, he hadn't particularly enjoyed it. They were notoriously unreliable, with a tendency to lose all reason just before the final cheque had cleared. But Scofield's voice had been steady and his eyes as clear as ice in December.

The only thing that seemed mad was his obsession with keeping his sister from mixing with strangers. He had presented it as a problem with a single inappropriate suitor. But she seemed to see herself as a victim of unjust incarceration.

If it was just a melodramatic attempt to gain his sympathy and turn him against his employer, it would not work. It was a shame to be on the wrong side of such an attractive young lady, but business was business. Despite what his mother might think, he was not being paid to flirt with the gentry, or to allow the gentry to flirt with him.

But it would have taken more strength than he had to look at Lady Olivia and not consider the possibility of a flirtation. Her eyes sparkled with intelligence but were the smoky blue-grey of clouds that seemed to hide her true thoughts as she'd stared at him. And though she wore her smooth blonde hair in a tight knot, he was sure that it would run through his fingers like silk, should he pull it free of its pins. Her body was a marvel of lush curves held in check by firm stays and a modest but expensive gown.

She was the picture of restraint, but he could see the fire burning in her, a passionate nature that must have alarmed her brother and caused his extreme strictures on her. She might pretend to be innocent, but she liked to sneak out of the house for liaisons with a man who was not yet her husband. If she would not protect her honour, someone must.

Was it only the one man, he wondered, or was this Clement fellow the last in a long line of indiscretions? His mind strayed for a moment, imagining her, bare in the moonlight, lips parted and arms open in invitation.

He closed his eyes tight against the fantasy. It did not matter how many men she might have known. She had made it clear enough just now that she had no interest in him as a man. It was not some mystical attraction that had drawn her to his side today. It was an upper class need to lecture an underling who appeared to be loafing on the job.

She was very nearly of age. If his job lasted more than a few months, he would be trying to contain a woman who had a legal right to choose her own husband. But even if he had the stupidity to offer for her, she would not be marrying him.

She would end up marrying someone very like the man she had chosen for herself. Mr Alister Clement had ample money and was from a decent family. He was even a member of the same club as Scofield and, though he had no title, he was welcome in the same so-cial circles. If Michael had had a sister, Clement was exactly the sort of man he'd want to marry her—stable, responsible and pleasant.

And since Michael's imaginary sister would likely be as illegitimate as he was, the proper Mr Clement would never offer anything so respectable as marriage. It made Michael hate the fellow just a bit more.

It also made him doubly glad that he was his mother's only son, for he did not want to see family behaving as foolishly as Olivia Bethune was, imagining herself in love when she just wanted to run away from home with the first man who would take her.

Of course, her brother was likely a mad killer. If the man's own sister did not trust him, then she was smart to want to get away from Scofield. And if Mi-chael discovered that her view of the situation was the right one…

He leaned back against the tree and tipped his hat back over his eyes. He would decide what to do if and when that moment came. In the meantime, he would do his job, just as he had promised, and make sure that Lady Olivia stayed where she was.

## Chapter Three

The last few days before the elopement seemed to crawl by in a blur of interminable hours and sleepless nights spent wondering if her escape might truly succeed. Liv avoided her brother as much as possible, sure that a chance word or glance would give away her intentions.

She also made no further visits to her new nemesis, Mr Solomon. Now that she had discovered who he was, she intended to ignore him, just as she had her other guards. She did not want to give him the impression that she welcomed the familiar way he spoke to her, or the smug way he smiled when he looked at her.

But she could not help sneaking glances out through the back windows of the house to see if he was still in the garden. It did not help that her bedroom, the morning room and all of her favourite rooms of the house faced the garden, or that it had always given her pleasure to be either in that space or gazing out at it. He was not like the previous watchmen, who had made every effort to be discreetly out of the way. Mr Solomon refused to be forgotten.

When she looked in the garden, sometimes he was there, other times not. She could find no discernible pattern to his schedule. It left her wondering where he might be when she could not see him. Was he at the front of the house? Inside it? Was he actually gone? Or was he standing right behind her?

Without intending to, she turned suddenly to look. Of course, she found nothing. She was quite alone. But in her imagination, she heard him chuckling in triumph. He had displayed such insufferable overconfidence when they'd spoken that he was probably still patting himself on the back over it, imagining her starting at shadows and brooding on their next meeting.

Thank the Lord, she would soon be seeing Alister, her comforting, predictable friend. He would take her away from this stifling house and she would never have to see Michael Solomon again. Strangely, the idea was not as exciting as it should have been. A part of her wished that he was in the garden right now, so she might go out and taunt him a bit before escaping triumphantly from his clutches.

The thought made her smile. She elaborated on it in her mind as she filled the basket on her bed with spare chemises and stockings, a journal and the string of pearls her mother had given her that she could not bear to leave behind. She was going to escape. For the rest of his life, Michael Solomon would obsess over her. She would be ever-present in his thoughts, the only woman who had bested him. Perhaps he would sigh, a trifle wistfully, that there had not been more between them.

She picked up the basket and walked to the kitchen, silently agreeing with him. It was a shame that they could not have spent more time together. Under other circumstances, they might have been friends. She would have enjoyed his banter had she met him at a dinner party and thought it more flirtatious than insulting. It had been a long time since a handsome man had got close enough to her to converse at all, much less tease her as audaciously as Mr Solomon had.

If Alister had a fault, it was that he was too plain-spoken and agreeable. He did not bother to toy with her when they conversed. He said his piece and she approved of it because he was a very sensible man. They talked about things, or rather he talked and she listened and nodded. But that was not quite so stimulating as having a discussion.

It was probably because their visits had been shortened by her brother's interference. Once they were married, there would be all the time in the world to converse and debate if they wished to. She smiled, imagining the marriage they would have. They would chat amicably over dinner, for they never argued. And soon the house would be filled with the laughter of children. It would be nothing like the silent tomb of the house she shared with her brother.

Now, she had arrived in the kitchen. And as they

did for her each week, the cook and her helpers had prepared a table full of baskets to take to the widows and orphans. Liv slipped her own basket onto the table beside them and looked up to see Michael Solomon standing on the other side, a heavily buttered slice of bread in his hand.

For a moment she could say nothing at all and had to resist the urge to snatch her own basket back before he lifted the cloth covering to see that it was full of ladies undergarments. Then she managed, 'What are you doing here?' The words came out in a high-pitched squeak and were the very opposite of the sound one wanted to make when one was totally innocent of mischief.

'I am trying to be of help,' he said with a benign smile, taking a bite of his buttered bread and backing into the path of a kitchen maid, as if to prove how utterly useless he had been so far. 'If we are to go out together, you cannot be expected to carry all of the baskets.'

'The footmen will carry them to the coach, just as they always do,' she said, then added, 'and we are not going out together. I am going with my maid, just as I always do.' Of course, it would mean going back upstairs and convincing her maid that her services were needed, after all. Today, she had taken great pains to convince the girl that no one would mind if she took the whole morning to nap and not just doze during the rides between carriage stops.

'It is of no matter to me whether the maid comes

or not,' Mr Solomon said, still smiling. 'The more the merrier.'

'It is not a question of whether or not *she* is needed,' Liv snapped. 'You are the one who is the interloper.'

Now, his smile was sympathetic. 'Then I will have to become accustomed to your dislike. For I am coming along, Lady Olivia. If it makes you feel better, I will ride on the seat with the driver.'

She gave an exasperated sigh. 'Do as you please, since it is apparent that I cannot stop you.'

He nodded happily. 'At last, we understand each other.' Then he gathered two baskets in each hand and walked out through the back door and around the corner of the house towards the waiting carriage.

The ride to the first stop was uneventful, as it usually was. The main difference came when they stopped and Mr Solomon jumped down from the driver's seat, taking the basket from her and walking behind her up the narrow stairs that led to the first widow's flat.

Liv was greeted with the same respect as always, along with a soupçon of curiosity directed at the unliveried man accompanying her.

She introduced him as an employee of her brother's. That statement would have been just as true of a footman. But it was clear, with Mr Solomon's charming smile and gentlemanly manners, that he was something more than a mere servant. The widows and grandmothers and impoverished maiden aunts they saw at each stop stared at him as Mrs Wilson did at her bag of boiled sweets, like a thing that could be savoured during the lonely evenings ahead.

In turn, he smiled back at them as if he was meeting the patronesses of Almack's, honoured to make their acquaintance and mindful of the time they spared from their busy day to take the baskets from him. He joked and they giggled like schoolgirls. He complimented and they blushed. They took no offence when he compared them to his own sainted mother, a handsome woman who was still very much in her prime.

Liv watched in silence, with a grudging respect for him. Though the initial plan in making these visits had been to meet with Alister, she felt a genuine concern for the ladies she visited. She could detect nothing false in Mr Solomon's treatment of them, and it was clear that they were enjoying themselves more than usual. Since they experienced very little in the way of happiness, she could not begrudge them this, even though it came from a source she did not appreciate.

But now they were coming to the last stop, and she was left with a dilemma. She doubted that she could convince him to stay with the carriage as she did her maid, for he showed none of the maid's usual signs of fatigue. But she had to make some effort to prevent him charging up the final set of stairs or he would ruin today's plan and prevent any future visits with Alister.

She racked her brain as the carriage came ever closer to their final destination, where her unsuspecting fiancé was waiting to take her away. There was no way to warn him of what was coming.

When the carriage slowed to a stop in front of Mrs Wilson's building, she leaned out of the window to announce to the footman that she was feeling far too tired to continue and requested that they start for home. But Mr Solomon had already hopped down from the driver's seat and was opening the door. 'Do not be faint of heart, Lady Olivia. I will help you up the stairs and carry your burden. You cannot leave a poor widow untended. And you have been doing such good work today. I am proud to be associated with you.'

'Thank you,' she said irritably, handing him the basket. It was no comfort that she had his good opinion, for that would change as soon as they entered the last building.

'Are you not going to take the last basket as well?' he asked, pointing to the one she had prepared for her elopement.

'I do not think it will be necessary,' she said. Perhaps it would be possible for Alister to overpower him. Then they could run for the back door. But Alister was not the sort to solve problems with brute force, and there was something about the set of Mr Solomon's shoulders that hinted he was quite capable of handling himself in a fight.

'Are you not bored with these endless stops?' she enquired, offering him a sympathetic smile.

'They are not endless,' he said. 'This is the last. But,

even if it was not, I have been having a delightful time, and have the strength for as many more widows as you can produce.' He gestured towards the house with his free hand. 'Lead on, my lady. I am yours to command.' This was in no way true, for he continued to refuse any direction that would make him stay with the carriage.

'I am quite capable of managing the last one myself,' she said. 'Mrs Wilson is very shy of strangers and might not welcome you.'

'I shall be on my best behaviour,' he said with a smile.

'I hate to put you to the trouble. It is really not necessary for you to accompany me to every stop,' she added, pulling on the basket he was carrying.

'On the contrary, I think it is.' He released the basket to her so suddenly the possession of it threw her off-balance. Then he preceded her up the stairs.

She hurried after him, mortified. He would discover Alister in the little flat, haul her back to the carriage and see to it that there were no more charity trips in her future.

Then Solomon glanced back at her with an expression that was far too wise.

He knew. Even worse, he had known all along.

She did not know how, but she was sure that what he would see when the door opened was exactly what he expected. She trudged resignedly behind him, allowing him to rap on the door.

When Mrs Wilson opened it she stared at him in suspicion, and Liv stepped quickly into the gap. 'We have brought your basket, just as always.'

'As always?' the woman said, glancing between the man in the doorway and the one who had started out of his chair in the corner, fists balled as if ready for a fight.

Solomon stepped into the room, beaming at the widow, as charming as he had been to all the others, and said in a loud voice, 'If you would do me the honour of introducing me to our hostess, Lady Olivia?' Then he glanced at Alister. 'And of course Mr Clement needs no introduction.'

Alister answered with a feral growl. It was clear that he did not know or care who Mr Solomon was, beyond realising that he was an obstacle to their plan.

Liv gave him a helpless look, then turned back to their hostess. 'Mrs Wilson,' Liv said, 'may I present Mr Solomon. He is an employee of my brother's, who will be accompanying me on my outings.' She glanced at Alister with another desperate look. 'Whether I want him to or not.'

'Charmed,' Solomon said, bending over the old woman's hand and making her chuckle.

Then he turned to Alister. 'And I am pleased to see you as well, Mr Clement. It was inevitable that we would meet since I was hired to prevent your elopement with Lady Olivia.'

Alister continued to stare at him in stony silence.

When he received no response, Mr Solomon went on. 'Although you may refuse to admit it today, a marriage between you will never be approved or permitted. If I were you, I would cut my losses and appeal to Scofield, who will probably offer a generous compensation should you surrender your plan and go about your business.'

'If I wanted money from Scofield, I'd have asked for it long ago,' Alister said, speaking at last. 'What I want is to marry the woman I love. No amount of interference on your part will prevent us from being together.'

The thrill of excitement that Liv felt at those words was diminished somewhat by the fact that the two men were so focused on each other that she might as well have not been in the room.

Mr Solomon stared back at Alister, his smile tight and the light of challenge in his eyes. 'Suit yourself, Clement. But if you have not managed to come up to scratch in all the time you've been courting her, I have little hope for you now.' Then he looked back at Liv expectantly. 'Will you have a seat, my lady? Unlike some in the room, I would not dream of taking the liberty myself, until you and Mrs Wilson are comfortable.'

Alister had not bothered to rise when she'd entered. But they had known each other for ages, and it was hardly necessary. Now, he sprang to his feet, but it seemed less a belated courtesy and more the first move towards a physical altercation with Mr Solomon.

Liv moved between them and turned towards the door. 'That will not be necessary, I am sure. It has been a long day for all of us. Now that the last package has been delivered, it would be best if we returned to Scofield House.'

Mr Solomon gave a nod of approval, and she glared back at him to prove that she might be going home as he wished but had made the decision without consideration for his feelings on the matter.

Behind her, Alister said, 'This is not over, Solomon.' She felt his hands on her shoulders and was spun around to face him. Then he kissed her roughly and with great passion. He released her just as suddenly, looking into her shocked face. He whispered, 'You will hear from me soon. Do not lose hope,' and spun her again, giving her a push towards the door.

She almost stumbled, but Mr Solomon was there to catch her, staring past her at Alister, his blue eyes darkened with sudden rage.

He relaxed again, releasing her to stand on her own, his smile returning. He turned back to Mrs Wilson, who was sucking a sweet and watching the proceedings as if they were a Covent Garden drama. He offered her a deep bow. 'Until we meet again, my dear.'

She gave him a toothless smile and clapped her hands, thoroughly satisfied with the way the day had gone.

Then he gestured Liv towards the door and, without turning, called, '*Au revoir*, Clement.'

As she took the first steps towards the street, she heard another growl from Alister and the door slammed behind them.

\* \* \*

As they returned to the carriage, Michael wondered if it might not be necessary to schedule another interview with the Duke to request a change in their arrangement. Now that he'd met Alister Clement, he was quite willing to forgo monetary compensation, just for the chance to plant a facer on the little twit.

He opened the carriage door for Lady Olivia and helped her up the step. Then he ignored the empty seat by the driver and helped himself to a place opposite her in the body of the coach.

She glared at him, casting her eyes towards the door as if she might will him back to his former place without a word.

He shrugged. 'Since you want to shout at me, it will be easier for both of us if I stay here.'

'Do not put words into my mouth,' she said. Then her mouth snapped shut as if to prove to him that she had no intention of doing what he expected, no matter how much she wanted to.

'Very well,' he said and stared at her, smiling, allowing the silence between them to build until she could not stand it any more.

'Why did you allow me to come on this trip, if you knew all along that I was going to meet Alister?'

'I was not absolutely sure,' he admitted. 'You had to be meeting him somewhere, and this was the most logical opportunity.' Though he had sincerely hoped that she would surprise him by proving him wrong.

'It was quite clever as well. Who would deny you the opportunity to do good works? I assume you came up with the idea.'

She nodded, and he thought he saw a faint flush to her cheek, as if she was happy that he had recognised her part in the ruse.

He nodded back. 'I doubt Clement has it in him to think so far ahead. How long have you been visiting Mrs Wilson?'

'Almost three months,' she said.

He smiled. 'You gave him the perfect opportunity for an elopement, and he waited too long to implement it.'

A shadow crossed her face as she considered the missed chance. Then she shook her head. 'He had his reasons, I am sure.'

'Are you?' he asked and watched the shadow reappear. He was not sure what excuses the man had given her, but they must not have been very convincing for it was clear she did not like to be reminded of them.

'You do not give him enough credit,' she insisted.

'And you give him too much,' he replied, then bit his tongue to prevent further criticism. He had been less than impressed with Alister Clement, a supposed gentleman, who had not bothered to greet his lover with basic courtesies and who pawed at her to prove his dominance in the presence of another man. But Lady Olivia would defend the fellow all the harder if Michael enumerated his flaws.

Now, she was looking at him with narrow-eyed suspicion. 'We cannot all be as clever as you,' she said, lips pursed.

She had not meant it as a compliment, but all the same he laughed. 'I thank you for that, but I suspect you are more than clever enough to be a match for me. It will be a pleasure working with you.'

'We are not working together,' she said emphatically.

'We are playing the same game, are we not? Just not from the same side of the board.' He smiled at her and leaned back in his seat, enjoying her beauty and the smooth ride of the Duke's carriage. He must not give in to the temptation of his mother's belief that there was a commonality between them. He was an interloper here, imposing on the lady's company rather than invited to share it.

But now she was staring at him with the same curiosity he felt about her. 'Is everything a game to you?'

'Not everything,' he said. 'Most jobs are puzzles, and not particularly interesting ones at that. Say I am called by a rich man to find the person responsible for the theft of his wife's jewels. Nine times out of ten, it is not some dramatic cat burglar that has done the deed. It is more likely to be a member of the family. I will find the stones at the nearest jeweller and be forced to cover up the discovery again, as the Lord pays back the insurance claim and punishes his second son.'

'That sounds very exciting to me,' she said, her eyes widening and her lover forgotten.

He leaned forward. 'It has left me thoroughly disappointed with human nature. So many of these cases would never occur if the family members understood each other.'

'And how are my brother and I any different?' she asked. 'I have no idea why he keeps me cooped up inside his house.'

'Perhaps he simply does not like Clement,' Michael said, stating the obvious.

'It goes deeper than that,' she insisted. 'The last man I was fond of was pulled out of the Thames with a knife in his back.'

'I beg your pardon?' he said, not sure he had heard her correctly.

'Perhaps you should look into the death of Richard Sterling before forming any opinions about my brother's motives,' she said, frowning at the floor.

'You think Scofield murdered someone?' he said, shaking his head.

'Other than the man everyone knows he murdered?' she replied, and her head snapped up to stare at him in frustration.

'The late Duke,' Michael replied with a shrug. 'People assume, of course. But there is no real evidence.'

'I was there that night,' she said with a shudder. 'I found the body…' She shuddered again. 'My father. And then Richard. That was when Hugh still allowed us some freedom to go about. But everything changed after Richard came forward with an offer. Hugh refused him, and two weeks later I read about his death in *The Times*.'

'Wait,' he said, holding up a hand in confusion. 'You had another suitor before Clement?'

She half shook her head as if the truth confused even her. 'There has always been Alister, of course. He asked my father and was refused. Then…' She swallowed as if she could not stand to speak of the murder again. 'When my brother became my guardian, both Alister and Richard asked and were refused. And Richard was…' She swallowed again, but this time a single tear rolled down her cheek.

'Oh, my dear,' he said, and before he realised what he was doing he had reached across the carriage to take her hands. They were cold and trembling and he covered them with his own, stroking gently to encourage the warmth back into them.

She took a deep breath and squared her shoulders, her voice hardening. 'I suppose I should be satisfied that he does not hate Alister quite so much as he did Dick Sterling. He has not bothered to hurt Alister, as of yet.'

'He would not have hired me if he had meant anything so nefarious as that,' Michael said, trying to smile and racking his brains to remember just what the Duke had said about the matter, upon hiring him.

*I want him gone.*

It had sounded firm at the time, a typical statement from a member of the peerage, as if people were furniture to be moved out of the way when they became inconvenient. Now, it seemed much more ominous.

Damn the man. If he'd meant murder, he should have said so directly, or done it himself. In either case, he should not have involved Michael in it. But, for the moment, the matter need not concern him. The worm, Clement, was more alive than he deserved to be, and Michael had no intention of changing that.

But he might be able to help the lady in front of him if he gave the matter some thought. 'Do not concern yourself,' he said, giving her hands a pat. 'You have only me to deal with, after all. And, although I cannot allow you to have the elopement you crave, I do not intend to do anyone permanent harm.'

'If you force me to remain in my brother's house, you are doing harm to me,' she said, pulling her hands away from him.

'No one is forcing you to remain with your brother. There will be other opportunities to leave, with other men, I am sure,' he said with a smile.

'I do not want another man,' she insisted. 'I am in love with Alister.'

'Love?' He could not help himself. He laughed again.

Her next breath left her in a hiss. 'How dare you doubt my feelings for him? What do you know about the matter?'

'I know that what you call love is nothing more than a combination of lust and expediency.'

'He has waited for me for two years,' she said with

an incredulous look. 'There is nothing particularly expedient about that.'

'You are a duke's sister,' he reminded her. 'It is unlikely that he could find a wife with a better pedigree. And you wait for him because he is the only man available to you. You want to get away from your brother's house. And Clement provides the logical method of egress. I suspect you would think yourself in love with any man who was willing to give you what you want. With luck, the next one will be someone your brother approves of.'

'You think me so shallow as to run away with any man who will have me?' She was glaring at him again, as she had when they'd first left the widow's rooms.

'Not shallow,' he said. 'Sensible. If I honestly believed you were in love with him I would be very disappointed indeed. He does not seem worthy of you, truth be told.'

'You could not possibly understand what this elopement means to me,' she said, turning away from him.

He could not stop himself from reaching out to touch her shoulder and turning her back to face him. 'You would be surprised at that, I am sure.'

'Oh, really?' She laughed, but there was no humour in it. 'Have you ever seen a murder, Mr Solomon?'

'I have seen many things that I would prefer not to remember.'

'But none of them were family, were they?' she pressed.

'No,' he admitted. 'Not family.'

'As I said, I was the one who found him,' she said, her eyes shut tight against the memory. 'Father was in the study, slumped over his desk. And the blood...' For a moment she was clearly overcome, pressing her fist against her mouth as if choking back a scream.

Again, he could not help himself and lurched across the carriage to take the seat at her side. Then he wrapped an arm about her shoulders, feeling her stiffen against him.

But the story continued to pour out of her, muffled against the lapel of his coat. 'I screamed,' she whispered, shaking. 'And Hugh came, and dragged me out of the room. They gave me laudanum and sent me to my room. But I could not stop seeing it.'

'That was two years ago,' he reminded her, stroking her back. 'There are no ghosts. It can't hurt you any more.'

'There might as well be,' she said with a weak laugh. 'I still have dreams. Nightmares, really. If something upsets me, if the weather is as hot as it was that night, the sight of blood...' She shook her head, trying to shake the memory out of it. 'And I am forced to live with the man capable of doing such a thing. I cannot manage to get away.'

His hand froze on her skin, aware of the truth she had spoken. She was trapped in the thrall of a murderer, and he was the one helping to maintain the prison. 'He has not tried to hurt you, has he?' Now his hand tightened into a fist and he thrust it into his coat pocket to hide it.

'He has done nothing at all. He has no patience for my spells. He barely speaks to me. And yet he will not let me go.' She shuddered. 'Until recently, my sister was there for company. She cared for me, at least. And she was always his favourite.'

'How would you think such a thing?' he said, not wanting to believe that there might have been a Bethune more fair than the one at his side.

'She was,' Olivia insisted. 'And now that we are alone? Sometimes, the way he looks at me…' She shuddered. 'He hates me. I know he does. And I cannot think why. I have never done anything to deserve it.'

'Other than trying to get away,' he reminded her gently.

'Any sane person would run from him,' she said, shaking uncontrollably now. 'I do not know why he wants me to stay. I mean nothing to him. He does not need me. My sister, Peg, said he claimed he never wants to marry. Perhaps he expects me to stay and be the lady of his house for the rest of my life. But what is the point of it when it is only the two of us there?'

He could think of several reasons why her brother might keep her cloistered, and none of them were honourable. 'But he has not hurt you,' he pressed.

'Not me,' she said, pulling away from him as if she had just remembered that she had a suitor. 'Alister is braver than you give him credit for. He has been willing to stand by me, even knowing who my brother is, and what he has done. And he has loved me.' She raised her head and gave him a watery smile.

'Of course,' he said, gritting his teeth. If Clement loved her as much as she thought, he'd have taken her out of this house years ago and rescued her sister as well. Instead, he'd found a million excuses to wait until the situation was most favourable to him and put her needs last. 'And I suppose you are still set on marrying him.'

She stared at him, her huge blue eyes still wet with tears, and nodded. 'He loves me,' she repeated. 'I have no mother. I have no father. Now that Peg is married, I have no sister. And now you are here to tell me that I have pinned my hopes on a man who wants me for my brother. Am I really so broken that you cannot believe a man like Alister would wait for me out of genuine and pure affection?'

'That is not what I meant,' he said. But neither did he want to explain the perfectly logical reason a man would be interested in a beauty like Olivia Bethune. Then he added in a gentler tone, 'There is nothing wrong with you, Lady Olivia. If anyone has a problem, it is Clement. He should have married you long ago. If…' He had been about to say, *If it was me.* But the comparison was pointless. It had not been him, nor would it ever be.

As if she could sense what he was thinking, she pulled away from him, sliding across the seat to put distance between them, and glared at him suspiciously.

'No one asked your opinion on the matter. And if you have been speaking nonsense to persuade me to cast him off, you are sorely mistaken. I am more determined than ever to become Mrs Alister Clement, and there is not a thing you can do to stop me.' Then she turned deliberately from him and stared out of the window for the rest of the trip.

## Chapter Four

Of all the horrible men that Hugh had hired to watch her and her sister, Michael Solomon was, without question, the worst. It was bad enough that he had found the time and place of their attempted escape. But that he had taken the opportunity to question her feelings for Alister was too much to bear.

The brief meeting in Mrs Wilson's sitting room had been a disaster. Alister was justifiably angry, and she'd had no time to explain to him that it was not her fault that they had been discovered. She was sure that she had done nothing to reveal the truth. But the kiss he had given her had felt more like punishment than love, as if he blamed her for what had happened. And though he had promised that it was not over between them, she was baffled as to when and how they would meet again.

Then Mr Solomon had been kind to her in the carriage. Between frustration and embarrassment and thinking of the night that she most hated to think about, she had been quite overwrought, near to tears. And then he had looked at her with such concern in his eyes. And he'd stroked her hands and promised not to hurt her, making her feel warm and safe inside. For a moment she had thought that somehow things might turn out all right.

Then he'd ruined it all. He had accused her of not loving Alister and grasping at any straw that might get her out of the house. For a moment she had thought he truly cared about what had happened to her. But then he'd proved that he had no heart.

She stared out of her bedroom window, down into the garden. He sat in his usual place beneath the tree pretending to doze but far more alert than she liked. He was wearing a neat grey coat that she knew would complement his eyes, should she go down to look in them.

For a moment, she actually considered doing so. It was lonely, sitting by herself in her room. She had read all the books in the library—twice through—and could not bear the thought of putting another stitch in her needlework. If she complained to her brother, he would remind her that they lived in a fine house, with all the servants she could wish for. There were many in London who would be envious of the ease of her life.

No matter how pretty, a cage was still a cage. She glanced again at Mr Solomon, who had spoken casually of chasing down jewel thieves. Of course, ladies never had such jobs as that. But it would be exciting to hear of such things when one's husband sat down to dinner. He had not said he was married, and she wondered if it would be impolite to ask. Just to satisfy curiosity, of course, and give a reason for conversation.

Of course, now that she thought of it, she did not like the idea of there being a Mrs Solomon and a family of attractive blond-haired children waiting at home to hear stories about the foolish rich girl he'd been forced to chaperone. She much preferred to think of him alone, as he was now.

There was a soft knock on her door and her maid entered, carrying a hatbox. 'Your new bonnet arrived from the milliner's,' Molly said with a smile, setting it down on the bed and stepping aside, eager to see the latest purchase.

'My new bonnet,' Liv said, confused. She did not recall buying such a thing on her last trip to Bond Street, nor were any of the previous orders unfilled. She was about to tell Molly to send it back when it occurred to her that a surprise package might be an excellent way for someone to get a message past her keepers.

She smiled and walked to the bed, untying the string and lifting the lid. It was obviously not something that she had ordered, for she'd have never chosen such a ghastly thing for herself. The band was too wide and covered in horrible red and white ribbon, with clusters of gillyflowers on either side of the brim. It was just the sort of thing that a man might select, if he had no notion of fashion.

Liv picked it up, glancing beneath it for folded note-paper or a message scrawled on the back of the receipt, but she found nothing. Then, as she picked it up and settled it on her head, she felt a lump behind a particularly garish red flower above her left ear.

She closed her fingers on it and turned her head to look at Molly. 'Isn't it the sweetest thing?'

'If you like it, my lady,' the maid replied dubiously, and dropped her eyes as if she couldn't stand to look at the thing a moment longer.

This gave Liv the opportunity to palm the crumpled paper, slipping it up her sleeve as she pulled the bonnet off and dropped it back in the box. 'You may put it away now. I will save it for a special occasion.' Perhaps on the day of her marriage, which she hoped would be revealed in the note she'd just found under the hatband.

The next morning, she stared up at the sky and the heavy drops that fell from it, shivering. It was looking to be a miserable day, and she was glad that Alister's planned escape was not scheduled until the following week.

Then, unable to help herself, she thought of Mr Solomon, sitting under the tree in the garden. Surely he would have the sense to take the day off and find somewhere dry to sit. Perhaps, if she promised him that she had no intention of running off today, he would find somewhere safe and warm.

That would be most foolish of her. If she could get him to go away, even for an afternoon, she should take advantage of the situation and leave. Knowing that, he would be a fool to budge, no matter the weather. It was unrealistic to hope for a truce, and she was not sure she even wanted one. Yet the thought of him out in the rain made her sad.

She was getting soft. Soft and foolish. She was not even sure he was there, yet she was worrying about him, even though he did not give a fig for her happiness. All the same, she found herself walking to the kitchen door and out, her shawl pulled up over her head to protect her from the rain.

He was there in his usual spot under the tree, an oil-cloth wrapped about his shoulders and rain dripping from the brim of his hat.

She spared him only a single glance before going to the dogs' kennel and calling, 'Caesar, Cleo, come.'

The pair of pugs raced past her and through the open door, where she could hear the rattle of collars and the shouts of the scullery maids as they shook off the rainwater on the freshly mopped kitchen floor.

Then she spared another glance for Mr Solomon, who was trying not to look enviously after the dogs.

'You'd best come too,' she said, jerking her head in the direction of the open door. 'I will not have you catching your death because of my brother's stubborn desire to keep me here.'

He was on his feet almost before she could finish the sentence. 'This invitation was not expected, but it does not in any way interfere with my mission.'

'If you were set to watch me,' she said with a shrug, 'you can do it inside just as easily as out.'

'More so,' he assured her. They were in the kitchen now and he was stripping out of his raincoat and hanging it on a hook beside the door. 'In any case, I would not recommend you attempt an elopement today. The roads will be impassable, and travel will be most unpleasant for all concerned.'

'Then for the moment we are at an impasse as well,' she said. 'There is a fire in the sitting room. I will ring for tea.' Why was she being so gracious to the man? He had done little to deserve it. But without a chance to go to the garden and banter with him, she would be spending the day in solitude. And rainy days such as this one always seemed to drag on, like an entire week forced into a single afternoon.

At least, with someone there, she would not be quite so alone. They followed the dogs down the hall to the sitting room and he immediately gravitated to the fire, holding his hands out to it, fingers spread as if to soak up all the warmth possible. He had not complained about his situation, but clearly he had been as miserable as the pugs.

When the housekeeper brought the tea she looked from one to the other of them, as if wondering if it was proper to leave the mistress alone with a strange man.

'It is all right,' Liv said with a sigh. 'If Hugh thought Mr Solomon was a threat to my virtue, he would never have hired him.'

The servant withdrew, and the man in front of the fire laughed. 'It is good that the rain has washed away what little pride I had left, or you'd have crushed the last of it.'

'Do you want to be seen as a threat?' she said, surprised. 'Because, if you are, I will have to send you back out to the garden.'

The wet dogs at his feet turned to her as if they understood, their little foreheads wrinkling with worry.

'No one is going back out in the rain,' she assured them. 'Not even the scoundrel you are protecting.'

'A moment ago, I was no threat. And now I am a scoundrel,' he said with a smile. 'Things are looking up.'

'Because you do not have the sense to be insulted,' she said, shaking her head and trying not to smile back.

'I cannot help the fact that I am a man,' he said, as if that should make sense to her. 'It is no compliment to think that you do not see me as such.'

'Because all men are threatening, I suppose,' she said, rolling her eyes at him.

By his silence, he probably thought this was the truth.

'Gentlemen are not,' she said, wondering if now he would be insulted that she did not think him one of those.

'That statement shows how few gentlemen you actually know,' he replied.

'I know Alister,' she said confidently. 'And he is no threat.'

Now it was Mr Solomon's turn to roll his eyes. 'He is not the yardstick with which to measure all of masculinity.' Before she could correct him, he added, 'You know your brother as well. He is as finely bred a gentleman as we are likely to find. Yet, from our conversations, I do not think you would call him harmless.'

He had trapped her. She should be defending both the men in her life, and yet she could not seem to find words to refute anything that he had said. Alister was meek and polite, and everything her brother was not. It was one of the things she liked about him.

Her brother was a murderer. And yet some part of her still loved him.

And Mr Solomon? Was somewhere between the two extremes. What was she to do about him? 'Are you saying I should not trust you?'

'Perhaps,' he said. 'Or perhaps I should not trust myself.' He glanced around the room, as if searching for a way forward. 'Now, what shall we do to keep busy until the rain stops?'

She looked at him, surprised. It had not occurred to her that she might be responsible for his entertainment if she brought him inside. Since she had not really planned to do anything more than stare out of the window, she could not really claim that his presence was interrupting anything.

'Chess?' she suggested, pointing at the board in the corner.

'An excellent idea,' he said, letting out a relieved breath. 'Black or white?'

'White,' she said, taking the advantage of the first move.

'And I will follow after, just as I do the rest of the time.'

The day was passing peacefully, and he was enjoying it. They had played three games already, a win each and a stalemate. It was a joy to find someone who was an even match in skill, for he liked a game to have a bit of unpredictability.

If he was honest with her, he should point out that the rain had stopped half an hour before. She did not have a good reason to keep him inside, nor did he have cause to stay. But the dogs were asleep, and it seemed a shame to disturb them. Now that he'd had the chance to talk to her about something other than her worthless fiancé, he found that Lady Olivia was actually quite good company. One more game would do no harm to either of them.

Then he heard a noise from the doorway. A cleared male throat, and the tap of a boot against the marble tiles of the hallway floor. He looked up to see the Duke watching impassively.

He looked back, making sure that his face was equally impassive and showed no trace of the guilt he felt.

He was afraid to look at the woman across the table

from him, especially after he heard her voice, too high and artificially bright. 'Hugh! You are home so early.'

Michael flicked his glance to the mantel clock, noting that it was nearly four. The day had flown by and they had not noticed the time passing.

'Not so early,' her brother said, his voice calm but his gaze suspicious. 'Were you not expecting me?'

'I'm sure your tea will be ready at the usual time,' she said with a weak laugh. 'Not that I have anything to do with the preparation of it.'

'And is this what usually happens when I am not here?' he said, raising an eyebrow.

'Chess?' she said with a strange inflection that made it sound like something forbidden. 'No. Not usually. I have no one to play with, being in the house alone.'

'But not today,' he said, staring at Michael.

'It was raining, you see,' she said quickly. 'And I did not have the heart to see Mr Solomon getting drenched to the skin.'

'Are you in the habit of watching him?' her brother asked.

It was an excellent question, and one that Michael should have thought to ask earlier.

'I went out to check on the dogs,' she said with a note of triumph, as if happy to light on an excuse. 'And I saw him in the garden.'

'And invited him in for tea and cakes,' her brother said in a disgusted tone, glancing at the empty cups on the table.

'Just until the weather improved,' she said.

'The sun is shining now,' he said in response. 'If Mr Solomon is finished playing games, perhaps he would care to note the fact from the window of the study.' Then he turned on his heel and left without bothering to see if Michael followed.

The Duke did not look because he did not have to. As an employee, of course Michael would go where he was expected to receive a dressing-down for being found in a place he never should have gone.

He turned and offered a sketchy bow to the lady seated before him, by way of an apology for leaving so abruptly. Then he turned and headed down the hall at a pace quick enough to catch the Duke at the door to the study, damning himself the whole way.

He could not decide what was the greater sin: to spend an afternoon chatting with his employer's sister, or to be caught doing so. Given the identity of the employer, getting sacked for not knowing his place was the least of his worries.

Once inside the study he stood like a soldier before a general, back straight, eyes forward, dead still, and waited for the explosion he was sure would come.

Instead, the peer took his seat behind the desk and looked up at him as if he were observing a specimen in a laboratory. Then he said in a dangerously ordinary tone, 'Do you enjoy your position here, Mr Solomon?'

He was ready to answer in the affirmative, then stopped, not wanting to sound as if he was taking too much pleasure in it, as it must have seemed in the sitting room. 'I appreciate it,' he said, which was a more accurate assessment. 'And I think, despite the way it might have looked just now, that I do it well.'

'Did I hire you to entertain my sister?' the Duke asked.

'No, Your Grace. You wanted to be sure that she was not eloping or forming attachments to inappropriate men. She was doing neither of those things today.'

'Do you consider yourself appropriate company for her?' the Duke asked. 'Because I certainly do not.'

The assessment was meant to sting, reminding him that he was nowhere good enough for a high-born lady. It was true, of course. All the same, he did not like having the fact rubbed in his face by his betters.

But pride was an emotion that he could not afford at the moment. So he replied, 'I was not thinking in terms of forming an attachment to her, if that is what concerns you. Nor do I fear that she is likely to become attached to me. I doubt she likes me very much, truth be told. But it will be easier to keep ahead of her if she views me as a confidant instead of a jailer.'

'That is good to know.' The Duke stared at him in silence until the air in the room seemed oppressive and Michael had to struggle not to turn towards the door. Then he spoke again. 'Because if anything inappropriate happens to my sister, you will pay with your life. Do you understand?'

'As Richard Sterling did?' he replied, unable to resist a counterstrike of some kind. It was the height of foolishness if the man was as dangerous as his sister claimed. But his research had turned up a story even worse than Lady Olivia's assumptions. Sterling had died shortly after a public argument with the Duke.

'What do you know of Richard Sterling?'

'Only what Lady Olivia tells me,' he lied.

'And what is that?' Was it his imagination, or did the Duke actually sound curious?

'That he was found dead in the Thames after his suit was refused.'

'He was not worthy of my sister either,' the Duke said with a strange smile. 'Sometimes, it is a wonder to me that Clement has lived as long as he has.'

'To me, as well,' Michael said, honestly puzzled at the man's reaction.

'If I were him, once this nonsense between my sister and him has been put to an end, I would take care to watch my back when walking by the river.'

'I will pass the message along, the next time I see him,' Michael said, fighting an urge to shudder.

'Very well,' Scofield said with another icy smile. 'You may go, Mr Solomon. You may go.'

## Chapter Five

Her second elopement was even more exciting than her first. Or perhaps nerve-racking was a better way to describe it. This time, she would be running away from the house, and must trust that Alister would devise a way to distract Mr Solomon and any other servants that might be watching her.

But he had given her no specifics as to how he was going to go about it. Five days had passed since she had found the message hidden in the bonnet, which had given her little more than the time and date and the instruction to run for the back gate when the moment came.

She was left hoping that he was as clever as her sister's husband had been in arranging their escape. At the very least, he must be more clever than Mr Solomon. And that man was not easily tricked.

So far, the pathway to freedom seemed suspiciously clear. He was not in the garden today, nor had he been there when she had sneaked outside in moonlight to hide a carpetbag of clothing in the dog kennel. What would happen if he reappeared just as she was trying to leave? He did not seem the sort that would pick her up and carry her bodily back into the house. If she saw him, she would remain firm and walk briskly past him, ignoring any objections. If he touched her, she would scream loud enough to bring the rest of the servants from the house and claim that he had accosted her for no reason. They would take her side against a stranger, and they would subdue him, giving her time to escape.

She checked the watch that was pinned to the bodice of her gown. It was one o'clock. The time had come. She waited for the expected sounds of a distraction, but none came. Perhaps it was a silent commotion, if such a thing existed. Alister had told her to leave at one, and leave quickly, no matter what she saw or heard. But she had not expected to hear nothing.

It seemed she would have to make the initial move, but it was difficult with nothing to signal the time other than the watch ticking against her heart. Perhaps it was because she had been waiting for so long that the act of rebellion seemed impossible. At the moment, her mind was making hundreds of excuses to delay.

She would be leaving her possessions behind, other than the few things she could manage to fit in the small bag already hidden. To the linen and pearls that had been in her basket the previous week, she had added a spare gown and a few books she was too sentimental to part with. After the way he had treated Peg when she had eloped, Liv doubted that Hugh would allow her back into the house to retrieve anything she had forgotten.

For luck, she had put on the ridiculous bonnet that Alister had bought to hide the note. They would likely laugh about that while on the road north. It would make for a pleasant story to tell their children.

The thought of children and a future made her smile. Unlike the prison she lived in now, her house would be full of laughter and love. She could imagine her husband smiling fondly at her as a little boy twined pudgy arms around her neck. She would soothe their nightmares just as they cured hers.

It was time to go. All she had to do was run down to the garden, grab the bag from the kennel and…

What would become of her dogs?

She had to admit that Caesar had done nothing to endear himself to the staff or to her brother. But he had been so much better now that he had Cleo for company. She even suspected there was another litter of pups on the way. Who would take care of them? Who would find homes for them?

She wanted to believe that her brother would not solve the problem by having a groom throw a squirming bag into the river. But, seeing how he had disposed of people in his life, she found it hard to believe that his sympathetic nature would suddenly appear when greeted by a half dozen extra dogs.

She shook her head, refusing to think of the worst thing that might occur. She was probably just making excuses to explain a case of cold feet now that the moment had come to finally strike out on her own.

But she would not be alone. Not really. She would be with Alister, who had waited long and patiently for the right moment that they could marry. Now that it was here, it would be most unfair of her to back out.

She paused in her thoughts, examining the last one. It almost sounded as if she did not want to marry Alister. And the fact that she did had been a thing she had been quite sure of for some time. She tried to imagine the happy future again and found that, while her beautiful blond children were easy to picture, it was much harder to imagine Alister as part of the family.

This was all Mr Solomon's fault. In the carriage on the way back from Mrs Wilson's, he had done everything possible to sow doubts, even going so far as to stroke her hands and stare sympathetically into her eyes. She must not let him turn her head.

She enjoyed spending time with Alister. She liked being kissed by him and had been looking forward to the greater intimacies that would come with marriage. Most of all, she liked the way he treated her, as if she were the most precious woman in the world. He loved her. And she… She took a steadying breath. And she loved him.

If she was hesitating, there was no logical reason for it. She had simply to put her fears aside, leave a note to the maid about the care of the dogs and run before Mr Solomon reappeared and spoiled everything. She scribbled a few lines, tied the ugly red ribbons on her bonnet, took one last look in the mirror and bolted down the stairs to the main floor and freedom.

No one stopped her as she left through the kitchen door without an explanation. And, surprisingly, no one bothered her as she reclaimed her bag and made her way through the back garden to the gate. Mr Solomon was still not in his place beneath the tree, nor had he bothered to lock the gate in his absence.

She laughed to herself. It was clear that Hugh had placed too much confidence in the man, probably in response to his arrogant manner. He might have been lucky on the first attempt. But when challenged a second time, it seemed he would be even easier to escape than his predecessors. She walked out through the gate and down the street to the corner, totally unhindered, casting an occasional glance behind her, still amazed at her luck.

The carriage was waiting, just as Alister had promised, out of sight of the house. He stood by the open door, waiting. 'I had begun to worry that you were not coming,' he said, glancing at his watch. 'We agreed on one o'clock.'

'It is only a little past that now,' she said, not bothering to check the time again. She could not deny that she had dawdled. But she doubted, after listening for years to her complaints about it, that he would understand how hard it had been to leave the only home she had ever known.

'It does not matter,' he said, patting her hand as he helped her into the carriage. 'Now that we are together, we will not have that problem again.'

She smiled back at him, not sure if she was relieved or annoyed. 'Of course not,' she said at last, giving him another smile.

'I have our trip perfectly planned,' he said, glancing out through the window. 'We will be out of the city within the hour, long before your brother discovers you gone, and will continue on the road north for six hours. We will be stopping at the Two Crowns, which is an inn known for its cleanliness and excellent food.' He checked his watch again, as if assuring himself that there was still time to make dinner. Then his attention shifted back to her as he consulted a notebook he pulled from his pocket. 'We will leave the inn at dawn, since we can assume that your brother will be mounting a pursuit—'

'What did you do to get rid of Mr Solomon, who was supposed to prevent all this?' she interrupted.

Alister laughed. 'Nothing at all. I came prepared, of course,' he said, raising his pocket flap to reveal the butt of a pistol.

'You meant to shoot him?' she said, shocked.

'Only to frighten him away,' Alister assured her. 'But it was not necessary. No one was there. It seems you have been worrying over nothing.'

'Oh,' she said quietly. She had been telling Alister for two years about the dangerous men that made an escape from the house impossible. But now that they had tried it, it had been easily done. It was one more reason to hate Michael Solomon. He had failed in his job and made her look like a fool.

But Alister was probably right that Hugh would send someone after them and confirm her fears. Of course, it should be Mr Solomon. If he was in any way competent, he should notice that she had gone long before her brother had and start his ride north only a few hours after them.

He would probably catch up with them at the first inn. When she had imagined this trip, she had given a lot of thought to the hours they would have to spend while passing the nights on the way to Scotland.

It would finally happen.

They would do the thing that lovers did, something she did not even have the nerve to name aloud. It would be legal, moral and common, after they were married. But while they were on the way to the marriage, there would be two, or perhaps three, very long nights. It was what she had been thinking about for almost two years.

But now that the time was almost upon her, she could not seem to stop imagining Mr Solomon bursting into the room a moment before things began and rescuing her. Her imagination was wrong. It would be an interruption, not salvation. She should not want to go away with him, just to be returned back to London and incarceration in her brother's house.

But in the scenario she was now picturing, when she

did not go willingly, he swept her up into his arms and carried her bodily from the bedroom. Her struggles against him were half-hearted, and soon she settled into his arms and clung to him.

Her mind searched the picture for Alister, wondering what he might make of it. But in her fantasy he was either absent or impotent, for he did nothing to stop what was happening. He was certainly not wielding a pistol to keep her at his side. He was simply not that sort of person.

'Olivia!'

Her mind snapped back to reality, and the exasperated man sitting across from her in the carriage. 'I beg your pardon?'

'You have not been listening to a word I've said, have you?'

In truth, she had not. But it had not seemed very important, when she had lost interest. She shrugged and smiled. 'It has been a rather overwhelming day.'

'Of course,' he said, smiling and patting her hand again. 'But now that we are on our way, you can relax. You have seen the last of your brother and his overbearing ways.'

'For a while, at least,' she said, taking a deep breath. 'Once we are married, perhaps he will relent and let us back into the family.'

Alister sniffed. 'Even if he does, I see no reason that we have to respond to the invitation. We will have everything we need, once we are together.'

She should be encouraged by that sentiment, for it was proof that Mr Solomon was wrong. Alister wanted her for more than her titled family and the allowance she might be provided. All the same, she could not imagine cutting Hugh, should he reach out to them. 'If not that, then perhaps I can see my sister again. Hugh prevented all contact after she ran away.'

Alister sniffed again. 'That was, perhaps, the only wise decision he made. Her choice of husband was not appropriate, nor was the way she ran off.'

It was strange that he would point a finger in the midst of their own elopement. But she chose to ignore it, focusing on his censure of Peg. 'She is my family, Alister, and I miss her most sorely. It can do no harm to locate her direction and exchange letters with her, if only to see how she is getting on.'

'We will discuss this later,' he said. 'There is no need to think of her when you should be focusing on your own honeymoon.' He smiled, as if the matter was settled.

She smiled back at him again, trying to ignore the feeling that, once they were married, he would have no reason to discuss anything with her. He would be the one making the decisions.

They progressed through the city slowly, which was the only pace possible in London traffic, and Alister spent much of his time staring out of the window, craning his neck to watch behind them as if, despite his earlier words, he expected the pursuit to be hot on their heels. After almost an hour of vigilance, he relaxed in his seat and stared across at her with an expression that she might have described as self-satisfied. 'It is finally happening,' he said, grinning again. 'After years of planning, you will finally be mine.'

They were just the words she'd needed to hear. He still loved her, no matter how long they'd waited. 'And you will be mine,' she added joyfully.

He laughed. 'Do not be ridiculous.'

Her smile faded. 'I did not intend to be. You are mine, just as I am yours.'

He gave her the sort of smile that one gave to frustrating children and shook his head as if he could not quite believe that he needed to explain. 'Possession is not a mutual thing, my dear. If it were, it would be terribly difficult to decide what belonged to whom.'

'That is true of objects, perhaps,' she said, glad that this was a simple semantic argument. 'But not when it comes to love. When we marry, I will give you my heart and you will give yours in return.'

'In a way, perhaps,' he said, still not convinced. 'But if we were having a proper church wedding, the matter would be much clearer to you. The vicar would ask, "Who gives this woman?" and your brother would hand you over into my keeping.' He frowned. 'If Scofield had not been so stubborn, that might have happened. Instead, I must steal you away.' He smiled again. 'In any case, you would not see a similar moment in the ceremony when anyone stepped forward to give me to you.'

It was true, of course. But she had never given the matter much thought. It was just as well, for if she brooded on the symbolism of the thing she might begin to feel as constricted as she did in the keeping of her brother. And never, in the years he had courted her, had she felt inhibited by Alister's affection.

'It is just as well, I suppose,' he added. 'For I could not think of a single person to stand up with me, should I need one.'

'I had forgotten,' she whispered, sorry to have reminded him. He had told her when they had met that he was an orphan and seemed so sad at the fact that she had been careful not to mention it again.

'But now I shall have you,' he said, smiling fondly at her and reminding her what it was that had made her come away with him in the first place. 'You shall be my family. It will be a new beginning.'

'For both of us,' she said, hesitating until he nodded in agreement. Then she broached the subject that had worried her before leaving. 'I was wondering, after things settle down, if we might persuade Hugh to part with my dogs.'

'Your what?' he said with a raised eyebrow, as if he had no idea what she was talking about.

'Caesar and Cleo,' she said with a small laugh. He was only feigning ignorance. Until Mr Solomon had taken to skulking about in it, they'd spent hours in the garden together playing with the pugs.

'Once you are married, you will have little time for them,' he said with a shake of his head.

'What will I be doing that will take the whole of my day?' she asked.

'Taking care of the children, of course,' he replied, as if it should be obvious.

'But, even in the best of circumstances, we will not have even one child for quite some time,' she reminded him. 'And the dogs do not need much entertainment. For the most part, they are fine keeping company with each other.'

'So you admit that you don't need them,' he replied, preparing to turn back to the window and end the conversation.

'It is not that I *need* them, exactly.' She wet her lips, hesitant to admit the truth. 'It is that I fear that Hugh might take some sort of revenge upon them, once I am gone.'

'Has he shown violence towards the dogs before?' He was giving her a look so reasonable that she felt irrational by comparison.

'It is not what he has done to the dogs that frightens me,' she said. 'It is what I know he is capable of.' Of course he had never harmed an animal, as far as she knew. But he had gone to great lengths to control her and her sister. 'Since he does not allow me to see other people, he must know that my dogs are my only company. If he has them, he might threaten them to try to get me to come back…'

Alister gave her a firm smile and a shake of his head. 'I will not allow you to go back. So it does not matter what he does to them.'

'But it does,' she insisted. 'I would feel so much better if I did not have to worry about them.'

And there was that smile, unwavering and obtuse. 'You will forget all about them in time. In any case, the point is moot. We will not have the space for a pack of dogs in our home.'

'I had not thought of that,' she said, cowed.

'I am not a duke, you know,' he said with a slightly bitter laugh. 'Once we are married, you will have to do without some of the frivolities you are used to. This is the first sacrifice you will have to make, and I am sure it will not be the last.'

'You are right, of course,' she said, trying not to let her voice quaver. 'I should not have bothered you.'

He gave her an approving look, satisfied that she understood.

Then, to lighten the mood, she tugged at the ribbon tied beneath her chin, undoing the knot and flipping the end in his direction. 'You have not complimented me on my new bonnet.'

He glanced up at it without a sign of interest or recognition. 'Oh, yes. Very nice.'

She was not normally the sort of girl to pout over a lack of compliments, but she could not help a small moue of displeasure. 'It is the hat you chose for me. The one that contained the note about this trip.'

'Oh,' he said again, giving it another look as if struggling to recognise it. 'I told the girl in the shop that any hat would do. Then I placed the note in it and told her where to send it.'

'I see,' she said in response. That explained a lot about the choice of decoration. He had not bothered to find something she might like. He had not even bothered to choose his own favourite. He had let a shop girl sell him a hat that no sensible person would take out of the shop. And now she was stuck wearing it for the remainder of the trip.

She glanced out of the carriage window, thoroughly tired of conversation. They were clear of the city now, the road wide and empty before and behind. The sounds and smells coming to her from the open windows of the coach were those of birdsong and hay, with the occasional whiff of horse along with the steady rattling of harnesses and clopping of hooves. As she listened, they seemed to slow, and she felt the sway and jerk as the carriage rolled to a stop. Then silence.

Alister tapped his stick against the front wall of the carriage hard enough that it might be felt on the back of the driver's seat. 'I say. Coachman. Hoy! What is the matter?'

No answer came, but she felt another swaying as the driver got down from his seat, probably to check on the horses. Still there was no sign that he meant to offer any explanation to his passengers.

Alister swore softly and reached for the door handle.

'Wait here. I shall go out and see what the matter is.' He offered yet another reassuring smile. 'It is probably nothing more than a loose shoe or a frayed harness. If so, I will give the fellow a good talking-to. He should have checked such things before we set out.'

He jumped out of the carriage and she saw him walk towards the front as the door swung shut behind him. The sound of muffled voices followed, then a single shout. And then she felt the carriage rock again as the driver remounted and the horses began to turn.

The vehicle swung in a wide circle and was heading back towards London by the time she had the presence of mind to call out of the window for Alister. Even hanging head and shoulders out of the window, she could see no sign of him on the road that was now behind her. He had to be back there somewhere, for he was not where he belonged, in the coach with her, nor did she think he was driving.

In the hour and a half that passed as she was transported back to London, her rage simmered, then boiled. She should not have been fooled at the ease with which she had escaped the house. She had underestimated Mr Solomon, so focused on his racing to catch her that she had never thought he might be some steps ahead.

A short time later they arrived back at the Scofield townhouse and Michael pulled to a stop at the front door. To any curious onlooker it would appear that Lady

Olivia was returning from a shopping trip and not an aborted run for the Scottish border. The day was devoid of scandal, and therefore a success.

He hopped out of the driver's seat and opened the door, smiling up at her before remembering that he had a muffler about his face to keep down the dust of the road and hide his identity. It had not been a particularly good disguise, but it had fooled Clement, who was the sort of man that gave little notice to the people working beneath him. He pulled it away, smiling again.

She responded with a glare. 'Where is Alister? What have you done with him?'

It was strangely disappointing that she still cared so much about a fellow who could not pull off a simple elopement. 'I have done nothing with him, Lady Olivia.' He could not help smiling a little wider at the memory. 'I did nothing that he did not bring upon himself, at least. He fell into that ditch with little help from me...'

'You pushed him into a ditch?'

'Not a particularly deep one,' he admitted. 'He was not injured, I am sure. He was rather wet, of course. And quite muddy. But otherwise unharmed.' Then he patted the pistol in his pocket. 'Unharmed and disarmed.'

'You left him defenceless in the middle of nowhere,' she finished, furious.

'A public highway in England is hardly the end of the earth,' he replied. 'He will have a bit of a walk before reaching the nearest house. A mile or two.' He thought for a moment. 'Three at most. Surely not four...'

'The middle of nowhere,' she repeated.

'He had his purse with him. I am sure he will be able to hire transport back to London, even if it is a cart ride from a local farmer.' Now he had to struggle to keep from grinning, which would further inflame her anger. 'The walk back to London might give him time to think about the wisdom of elopement.'

'I don't want him to reconsider,' she said, shaking her head. 'Alister has been the only constant in my life through all the difficulties. If he leaves me…'

He offered her a hand to help her from the carriage and his fingers tightened on hers in an encouraging squeeze. 'Then you will marry a man who is more worthy of your affections.'

For a moment her hand responded to his touch, clasping his. Then she yanked it away and grabbed the carriage door to help herself to the ground. 'What makes you think that I had not found such a man in Alister?' she demanded. 'Just what is it about him that you find so objectionable?'

He paused again, then glanced at her head. 'Perhaps it is his taste in millinery.'

She snatched the bonnet off her head, threw it to the ground and stomped on it with a silk-slippered foot. Then she glared at him. 'If anyone had reason to object to this abomination, it was me. But you did not see me shoving anyone into a ditch over it.'

'Of course not,' he replied, hoping to calm her.

'No,' she said, dragging the word out until it sounded

like a bitter laugh. 'I wore the thing. Out of love for the man who gave it to me.'

He was afraid to point out that snarling a declaration of love was not likely to convince anyone of her feelings. Instead, she looked and sounded as if she wished Alister might be here to meet a fate similar to that of his hideous bonnet.

He scooped up the crushed hat from the ground and let one of his arms hover about her shoulders to shepherd her towards the front door. 'Let us go inside and we can discuss this further.'

'If my brother weren't mad, then perhaps I would not have to sneak off to Scotland with the only man who has asked,' she said in a tone that said tears were not far away.

'There, there,' he added, unsure of what else could be said. But he was sure his employer did not want the family discussing his sanity on the street in front of the house. He let his arm drop to touch her shoulders, drawing her forward and staring daggers at the footman, who was gawping through the window instead of opening the door.

When they reached it, he opened it himself, dragging her through just as the flood of tears arrived. He gave her back an ineffectual pat, which only seemed to encourage her to lean into him, clinging like a vine in sight of the butler and two parlour maids. He shot them all a helpless look and mouthed 'Tea!' over Lady

Olivia's bowed head, then led her towards the sitting room and shut the door.

'If my sister Peg had not run away, she would not have been allowed to marry at all. If Hugh wished to see us married to proper men that he could accept, he could just as easily have found us husbands. Instead, he hires men like you to follow us wherever we go and make sure that we never meet anyone.' At the moment, she did not seem to be too bothered with him in particular, since she was muttering her complaint into the silk of his waistcoat.

He squared his shoulders, squared his jaw and tried not to be moved by the nubile beauty sobbing in his arms. 'Be that as it may, following you around is the job that has been set to me and I will do it to the best of my ability.'

She grimaced. 'You searched the hatbox and found the note,' she said with another sob.

He nodded and patted her back, reminding her, 'It is my job to anticipate your actions and respond to them.'

'I hate you,' she said. The tears came faster but she made no attempt to move out of the circle of his arms.

'I know,' he replied, closing his eyes and trying not to focus on the feeling of her body shuddering against his.

'I hate Hugh as well,' she said on another sob. 'And Alister.' This last was delivered on a wail of misery.

*Well, that is some progress, at least.*

It took an immense amount of restraint not to announce his true feelings.

When he did not answer, she announced, 'I hate all men.' There was a hysterical tinge to her crying, as if she would never stop. He might be trapped here for ever in this impotent embrace, holding a woman who had no idea what she was doing to him. She was a sweet armful and, despite what she might think of someone hired to keep her safe, he was a flesh and blood, human male who could not be expected to ignore his feelings indefinitely.

And so he showed her. He pushed her away so he might see the shocked look on her face before pulling her back in for a kiss that was wet and salty, and open-mouthed confusion. He came to his senses at the first touch of her tongue and pulled away again, trying to look more composed than he felt.

She was staring at him with those enormous blue eyes, her fingers raised to touch her lips as if she expected to feel a change in them.

It occurred to him that he should say something. An apology was probably necessary. But no amount of sorrow would save him if she decided to tell her brother what had happened. In any case, he was not sure he regretted what he had done. After two years sneaking about with Clement, it was not as if she was an innocent schoolgirl who would be ruined by a single kiss.

The silence between them grew long and embarrassing and, unable to think of a better way to end it, he clapped his hands together in a gesture of completion and said, 'There. Now that you have stopped crying, I will go and see what is keeping your tea.' Then he hurried out of the room to find the housekeeper.

## Chapter Six

'Another cup, Lady Olivia?' The housekeeper was hovering, justifiably worried about her state of mind.

'No, thank you,' she said, annoyed at the way her cup rattled in the saucer. The situation called for something stronger than tea. 'Would it be possible to have a small glass of ratafia? Just as a restorative. It has been a long day.'

'Of course, Lady Olivia.' The housekeeper returned a short time later with a large glass of what they both knew was straight brandy flavoured with sweetened fruit. But since Hugh thought it was a delicate drink fit only for ladies, he would not question her desire that the servant leave her the pitcher.

Liv took a deep sip and felt her tongue go numb. It was an improvement on the way her mouth had felt before, when it was still wet from Mr Solomon's kiss. He had only done it to stop her from crying. She supposed it was better than a slap in the face, but that at least would have been easier to recover from.

Had Alister even bothered to kiss her when she'd got into the carriage? She could not seem to remember. If he had, it had been a thoroughly forgettable kiss and totally unlike the one Mr Solomon had given her, which had seared her to the soul.

The door opened and Hugh entered, staring at her with a look of concern. 'Olivia, are you in distress? They sent a footman to fetch me.'

She fumbled with her drink before remembering that she had nothing to be embarrassed about. 'Do I look distressed?' she said, taking another drink of her brandy.

'The servants said you were crying. If it is something that Solomon did, I'll…'

'No,' she said, holding up a hand to prevent him from finishing the sentence. 'I might as well tell you the truth, for he will likely report it to you tomorrow. He did what you wanted him to. He stopped me from eloping with Alister.'

Her brother gave a satisfied smirk. 'And what became of Mr Clement?'

'Left in a ditch on the road to Birmingham.'

At this, her brother let out a bark of laughter.

Liv took another deep drink and resisted the urge to laugh along with him. But that was probably from the effects of the brandy and had nothing to do with her feelings for Alister.

Hugh gave her a searching look, as if he could read the details of what had just occurred and expected her to admit all. 'And how are you getting on with Mr Solomon?'

'Fine,' she blurted, feeling her cheeks go pink. 'By that, I mean he is as annoying as all the other men you have hired to harass me.'

'I see.' His answer was as opaque as his expression. 'Then you will be giving him no more trouble?'

She took another drink, holding the glass with both hands to keep from trembling. 'Do you plan to release me from this house?'

His mouth tightened until his lips were a straight, stern line. 'What I do, I do for your own good. Until I am sure you do not mean to do anything foolish, I cannot give you more liberty than you already have.'

'I have none at all,' she said, draining her glass and pouring another. It would serve him right if she took to drink to pass the empty hours. Or she could reveal what had just happened with Mr Solomon and have the man fired. Then she could take advantage of the confusion to escape again. All she had to do was speak and she was one step closer to freedom.

She stared at her brother for a moment, considering. Then she said, 'Since there is no point in speaking further with you, I will take my glass and retire to my bedroom, where I can never get into any trouble at all.'

It was the brandy talking, she was sure. But the shocked look on her brother's face made her happier than she had been all day.

The next morning she woke in a foul mood with an aching head and an empty decanter on the bedside table.

But excess had done nothing to chase away the doubts raised by her elopement. Nor did she understand how she felt about Michael Solomon.

Why had he kissed her? Why had she let him? And what was she to say to him when she saw him today?

She did not have to say anything. She would not have to talk with him if she did not go into the garden. She would not see him if she did not look out of the window. Better yet, she did not have to be in the house at all. If she was properly chaperoned, Hugh had no objection to her taking occasional excursions to Bond Street. Although she'd thought she had a surfeit of it on the coach trip yesterday, a little more fresh air would do her good.

She notified Molly that she wished for a walking dress, and that she would be required to come along to prove to Liv's keeper that she meant no harm. Then, dressed and fortified, she walked down the stairs to the front door, her maid trailing behind.

She made it as far as the foyer before being stopped by Mr Solomon. He smiled at her as if surprised by her impending departure, but she was beginning to believe that nothing she did truly surprised him.

'Where do you think you are going?' he said, still smiling, but standing in front of her to block the door.

'I am going shopping,' she said, tightening the ribbon on her bonnet with a jerk to show him that she was in no mood to be trifled with.

'Correction,' he replied. '*We* are going shopping.'

She wondered if he took pleasure in dashing her

hopes or merely liked arguing with her. 'You do not need to accompany me,' she said, moving to go around him. 'I will be taking Molly with me and need no further chaperone.'

'The maid who accompanied you when you visited Mrs Wilson?' He shook his head and turned to the girl. 'You will not be needed, my dear. I will chaperone your mistress.'

The maid gave her a confused look, then turned towards the stairs.

'Do not listen to him,' Liv said in a sharp tone. 'You are my servant.'

'Actually…' Mr Solomon said with a dramatic pause, 'it is Scofield who pays your wage.'

Molly gave her another desperate glance before deciding that, by extension, she must obey Mr Solomon. Then she ran for the stairs, disappearing up them before Liv could mount further argument.

Now she was stuck at the front door with the very person she had been leaving the house to avoid. 'I do not actually have to go shopping,' she said.

'Women rarely have to do it, though they seem to like it well enough.'

'I am not going to meet Alister, if that was what you were assuming,' she said.

'I am not assuming anything,' he replied, 'though it would be an excellent opportunity to do so.'

'I just cannot stand to be in this house another minute,' she said, squeezing her reticule as if she wished to choke the life out of someone.

'Then by all means let us go,' he said, eyeing the purse nervously. 'A brisk walk will do you good. I will stay a step or two behind you and say nothing. It will be as if I am not even there.'

She gave him the most imperious look she could manage then swept past him, out through the door.

As he had promised, he followed, out of sight but never out of mind. She could not help feeling that he was watching her as she walked, which made her strangely aware of the sway of her hips, a thing she had never thought about before.

Now that she was concentrating on it, she could not seem to decide if she was walking correctly. Too much swing would be a flounce and might look as if she were trying to get his attention in a most common way. Too little left her walking stiff-legged, as if she had something wrong with her knees. There had to be a happy medium somewhere between the two that she used when walking normally. But, try as she might, she could not seem to find it.

'Excuse me, Lady Olivia?'

'Yes,' she said with a sigh, not turning to look at him.

'Do you have a stone in your shoe? If you are in distress, we could stop…'

She did stop, so suddenly that she heard him stumble behind her while trying to maintain a proper distance between them. Then she turned and looked back at him, trying not to be intimidated by the nearness of him, or the way she had to look up to see his face. 'Have you ever been followed, Mr Solomon?'

He considered for a moment. 'On several occasions. A memorable example was the time a pair of cutpurses tried to trap me in a blind alley. It did not go well for them,' he added.

'If you have, then you will know that it is useless for either of us to pretend that I do not know you are there. Your presence is…very distracting.'

At this declaration a slow smile spread across his face, as if he understood exactly what her problem was. Then he replied in a voice that was polite and professional, 'I cannot leave you alone. My job would prevent that. But there is no reason that I cannot walk at your side, if it does not offend you.'

'Very well,' she said with a sigh. It was hardly an improvement but, short of running back to the house like a coward, she could not think of a better solution.

They walked in silence for a while, which gave her too much time to brood on the happenings of the previous day. 'Mr Solomon.'

'If you are about to ask me about the kiss, it was a mistake. Nothing more than that. I know that my infringement on your person was inappropriate and I sincerely apologise. You need not worry that it will happen again.'

It seemed that his mind had worked much the same as hers did, when left with too much silence. That was some comfort, at least. Although he had been awfully quick to deny it just now. She agreed with him, of course. But a moment of wistful hesitation would have been a salve to her pride.

'You were crying,' he said, filling in the silence she had created, as if it made him uncomfortable. 'And I am hired to solve problems.'

'You viewed my display of emotion as a problem?' she said, more interested than surprised.

'It was something that needed fixing,' he said. 'And the kiss put a stop to it.'

She sighed. 'That is very like a man.'

'I should hope so,' he said. 'I am male and can be expected to behave as one.'

'I did not mean it as a compliment,' she said, narrowing her eyes in his direction, then looking straight ahead again.

'Then exactly what did you mean?'

'The tears were not the problem. They were a reaction to the problem. In stopping them, you did not solve anything more than your discomfort at their presence. My problem still remains.'

He thought for a moment, then said, 'I see.'

'The trip out of the house is making me feel a bit better,' she admitted. 'It would be improved if you were not following me, of course.'

'Of course,' he agreed, not bothered by the statement.

But had it been true? She was not sure. At the moment, his company was not bothering her in the least.

And it was good to have someone to talk to who had more sense than Molly.

'Do you like working for my brother?' she asked, to remind herself that he was really not that much different than the maid.

'He pays well,' Michael said absently. 'And promptly. That is better than much of the peerage, who seem to think that their patronage is some sort of honour that does not require compensation.'

'But do you enjoy what you are doing right now?' she said. It would be foolish of her to convince herself that this was a normal conversation when he was only here because his job required it.

He considered again. 'He has not asked me to do anything that would violate my personal code of honour. Though you do not want me to follow you about the town, it is more an inconvenience to you than actual harm.'

'True,' she admitted.

'And I have been asked to do more difficult things than escort a young lady down Bond Street and stand meekly by as she chooses ribbons. So, today at least, I enjoy working for your brother.' Then he smiled at her in a way that went far beyond professional courtesy.

She held her breath for a moment, then asked about the thing that most troubled her. 'When you have spoken to him, has he given any indication that he might be unstable?'

The pause that followed was a trifle too long. 'No

more so than any other jealous older brother,' he said, then added, 'and I hope you do not tell him about this. I doubt he would understand.'

'It will be our secret,' she said. If, as she suspected, he was lying about her brother to protect her feelings, she did not dare let Hugh suspect that there was anything between them. Though Mr Solomon seemed to be able to take care of himself, she did not want to see him end up like Richard Sterling. She glanced at him again, remembering the feel of his lips, and could feel herself blush.

'Now, what is it that you wish to get?' he said, pretending not to notice her interest.

They had reached the shops, and she looked around her, unsure. The intent in leaving home had never been to make purchases. Then she thought of the bonnet she had destroyed yesterday, and went to a milliner's, and then another. After enough dithering to drive any gentleman mad with frustration, she chose a bonnet dressed with blue ribbons and delicate forget-me-nots.

When she went to hand it to the shop girl, she turned to her companion.

Instead of yawning in boredom, Mr Solomon gave a nod of approval.

'You like my choice?'

'The blue suits you well,' he said, as if the matter should be obvious. 'The flowers bring out the colour of your eyes.'

She glanced in the mirror again, looking at her own

eyes. Of course, she was aware that it had looked well on her. But it was a surprise that he could tell what colours flattered her, when it was clear after yesterday's discussion that two years had made no such impression on Alister. 'It should not be your business what colour suits my eyes,' she said, annoyed.

'True,' he replied. 'But I would be lying to claim that I had not noticed that they are a very lovely blue.'

He had looked at her eyes. The thought made her blush again, for it was another proof that he viewed her as something more than just a nuisance. 'And I suppose you have formed an opinion about my dress as well.'

'Though some colours might favour you more than others, even the plainest of gowns does not diminish your beauty,' he replied. 'But surely you are aware of that.'

In truth, she was not. It had been so long since she had worn a ballgown that she had almost forgotten what she looked like when she was trying to impress. Though Alister had told her that she was pretty, he did not usually waste the time they shared with compliments. And she doubted her brother noticed her at all. 'It is kind of you to say so,' she said, her face downcast. Then she peered at him through her lashes, less in an effort to flirt than out of fear of looking directly into his eyes.

They stepped out onto the street and he held out a protective arm as a shop boy ran past, almost colliding with her. Then he held out his hand for her package, showing no sign of embarrassment at the prospect of carrying a lady's hatbox. During her brief time with Richard, he had been far more interested in telling her about himself than he had in hearing about her wants and needs. Alister was better than that, but the closer she got to marriage, the more it seemed that he would be deciding their likes and dislikes and making all the plans for both of them.

She looked up at Mr Solomon, who was guiding her across the street towards a parfumier's, watching out for traffic and keeping her clear of the muck of the street. He was so kind and so helpful, and not the least bit annoyed that she chose their route.

And then she remembered that none of it was a matter of affection. He was paid to keep her out of trouble. Apparently, the best way to do it was to flatter her eyes and cater to her every whim. The kiss that he had given her yesterday was part of the job as well.

She was about to tell him that none of this was necessary when a voice sang out from the pavement ahead of them.

'Michael! Michael! Yoo-hoo!' An attractive woman was bustling towards them, furiously waving a handkerchief to get Liv's escort's attention. Though he was a handsome man who had garnered more than his share of female attention from the girls they had passed, this lady was a trifle old to be casting after someone like Michael Solomon. There were threads of silver in the blonde curls peeping out from under her bonnet. And she could not have been interested in courtship for the hat was a widow's deep black, as was her stylishly cut pelisse, decorated with jet beads.

Though she was dressed for deep mourning, her mood was happy enough and her style was of the latest mode, as if to show that while she might not wish to look for a husband, she was not so lost in grief that she did not want men to notice her. But the man she was waving at winced and turned deliberately away, pretending not to see.

Liv smiled, surprised to see him so put out, and grabbed him by the arm, forcing him to turn back the way they had come, towards the strange woman. 'I think someone is looking for you.'

'She should not...' he muttered, then added more loudly, so that the woman could hear him, 'I am working.'

'I do not mind,' Liv said with a laugh, slipping her hand into the crook of his arm. 'It would be terribly rude to cut her in the street.'

'Michael,' the woman said, puffing slightly at the exertion of catching them up, 'I never expected to see you here.'

'Because I am on business,' he said. When he spoke, his lips barely moved, as if he wished it were possible to make the whole situation pass without having to speak at all.

'And who is this charming creature you are escorting?' the woman said, beaming at Liv. 'You have never mentioned her, I am sure.'

'I mentioned her at breakfast, just the other day,' he said, giving the woman a warning look.

Liv raised her eyes in surprise, for clearly the two were better acquainted than she had assumed. The fact that either of them would mention breakfasting together was truly shocking.

Michael immediately realised his mistake and announced, 'It is not as it sounds.'

The other woman huffed and rolled her eyes at him. 'Really, Michael, you must acknowledge me now, if only for the sake of my honour.'

'By all means, Michael,' Liv said, goading him onward. 'Enlighten me.'

'Lady Olivia Bethune,' he said, teeth gritted. 'May I present Mrs John Solomon. My mother.'

The widow Solomon dropped a curtsey. 'Delighted to meet you, Your Ladyship. You are the sister of the Duke of Scofield, are you not?'

'The eldest of his two sisters,' Liv supplied.

'He might not have told you, but Michael has a charming house in Cheapside, on Gracechurch Street, with space enough to take in his poor mother so that she does not need to be alone.' She said this with a twinkle in her eye, as if, even were she not living with her son, she was unlikely to be too lonely.

'She is not interested, I am sure,' Mr Solomon said, glaring at his mother.

'On the contrary,' Liv replied. 'I am fascinated. Your son has told me very little about his personal life.'

'Because it is none of your business,' Solomon snapped, then blanched with embarrassment. 'I do not normally discuss my work when at home,' he said. 'Particularly not when it involves a gentle born lady.'

'He did not give me any of the details,' his mother said with a dismissive wave of her hand. 'I worked those out for myself. You are the heiress that is trying to elope against her brother's wishes?'

Liv could not help smiling, for Mrs Solomon's cheerful nature was infectious. She dropped a modest curtsey and said, 'None other. And your son tracks me like a bloodhound each time I leave the house.'

Mrs Solomon put her hand to her heart in a dramatic gesture of surprise. 'Your brother is a heartless man if he insists on standing in the way of young love. But then, we all suspect the worst of him,' she added in a whisper.

'Mother!' Liv did not have to look at Mr Solomon to know that he was horrified by his mother's comment.

'It is all right,' she said softly. It was almost a relief to finally hear someone say aloud what everyone must think when they saw a member of her family. She smiled at Mrs Solomon. 'It is not easy, being the sister of the Duke of Scofield.'

'Well, I am glad that he is allowing Michael to walk out with you,' she said with a nod of approval.

'He is not allowing me to go about with her,' Michael said, a hint of desperation in his voice. 'I have been hired to watch her.'

His mother glanced down at the hatbox in his hand. 'Of course, dear. I am sure that is all it is.'

Liv tried not to giggle. It was clear that the poor woman had aspirations on behalf of her son. 'He is only trying to prevent me from eloping with another gentleman. Our shopping trip is a distraction.'

'Of course, my dear,' the other woman said, reaching out and patting her hand. 'If you have your heart set on another gentleman, then by all means run to Scotland. You will not regret it.'

'Do not listen to her,' Mr Solomon muttered.

'My Mr Solomon and I eloped, and it was quite the thing.' His mother gave a heavy sigh. 'He is gone now, alas. Since shortly after Michael was born.'

'And you still mourn him,' Liv said, looking at the black dress. She had assumed, from the full mourning the woman wore, that the loss was much fresher.

'A love like ours could never be repeated,' Mrs Solomon said with another sigh. 'He was very gallant, and we were very much in love.'

'Enough!' her son announced. 'Lady Olivia does not need to hear your stories.'

'That is all right,' Liv said, surprised at his anger now that the conversation had finally turned from her and her family. 'I do not mind.'

The woman smiled at her fondly. 'You are too kind. Michael has heard it all too many times to be affected by it. But I was once young and in love and understand the desire to follow your heart, despite what family may say. Trust me, my dear, if this is what you truly want, you will find a way, no matter what Michael might do to stop you. I disobeyed my parents and, despite all that happened after, I never regretted it for a moment.'

'Not another word,' Michael said in a warning tone.

His mother sighed and looked to her son. 'Very well, I will leave you to your *business*.' Then she smiled at Liv and winked. 'And I wish you luck on your impending marriage. But if it does not work out, then you might consider looking right under your nose.' She drifted away as her son turned a violent shade of red.

Liv looked after her. 'That was very interesting.'

'It was nothing of the kind,' he barked, turning and walking hurriedly down the street as if he'd forgotten that he was meant to be following her.

She hurried after him. 'I never thought about you having a mother.'

'Did you think I sprung full blown from the head of Zeus?' he said, staring back at her in amazement. 'Of course I have a mother. Everyone does, whether they like it or not.'

'I mean living,' she said, immediately feeling foolish. 'And living with you,' she added.

'It is not as if I would put her out in the street,' he said, looking over his shoulder at his mother's retreating back as if he might wish to do just such a thing at this moment.

'My mother is dead, of course,' Liv added. 'She was

lost birthing Peg. I cannot tell if I remember her or have imagined what I wanted her to be.'

'Well, mine is alive,' he said, his shoulders set defensively. 'And, for all I know, my father is alive as well.'

'But your mother...' Liv made a gesture to encompass the drama of his mother's full mourning dress.

'There is no John Solomon,' he replied, his mouth set in a bitter line. 'When I was old enough to notice that her stories changed depending on her mood, I set out to look for him. The Solomon family turned me away at the door when I asked after him. There is no record of his death or their wedding, other than the mention of him on the church register as being my father. And she could have written any name in that spot.'

'But that would mean...' she said, surprised.

'That I am a bastard. Either John Solomon's or someone else's. And that my mother made up an elaborate story to save face after I was born,' he completed. 'My mother received regular payments to cover the cost of my upbringing and tuition at a decent school. But I have been unable to find the source of them. Her family was no help at all and slammed the door in my face when I came to them with questions.'

'So that might mean that she has been in mourning for a man who does not exist,' she said, embarrassed that he was revealing such details.

'She has worn black for twenty-nine years to hide the truth,' he said with a bitter quirk of his lips. 'She is quite mad, you see.'

'All the same, I enjoyed speaking with her,' Liv said, still finding it hard to believe that there was anything odd about the woman they had met. She seemed not just ordinary, but quite charming.

'She has been fostering the delusion for so long that she cannot tell it from reality,' he said, shaking his head. 'And the fact that she would hint that you and I…'

'She is a proud mother,' Liv replied, wondering that, even after kissing her, he found the prospect of the two of them together to be so unlikely.

'She was talking nonsense,' he said gruffly. 'And, unlike her, I know my place, which is so far beneath you as to make a connection between us impossible. Your brother would be appalled to think that I was mistaken for anything else but a footman.'

'My brother does not enter into this conversation,' she said, not wanting to consider what might happen if Hugh found out that she considered this man a friend or, perhaps, something more.

'I am happy to hear you say so,' he said with a sharp laugh. 'If you want to be rid of me, all you need to do is tell him how I behave when I am near you.'

'All that would accomplish would be to see you replaced with another, whose company I do not enjoy half so much.'

She had been too frank. He was looking at her now, silent and intrigued. The air seemed to crackle between them in wordless communication.

'None of the other men my brother has hired have

such excellent taste in bonnets,' she said, breaking the connection between them.

He laughed, to acknowledge the jab and allow them both to pretend that nothing had happened. But there was something in his eyes. Was it wistfulness or regret? It passed so quickly that she could not tell. Then he turned, ready to lead them across the next street.

They were barely off the kerb when a horseman seemed to appear out of nowhere. The stallion he was riding was out of control, snapping and kicking, first with front legs, then back. Mr Solomon turned to her, shoving her backwards and tossing her hatbox after her as the horse bore down on him, knocking him to the ground.

## Chapter Seven

'Are you sure you are all right?'

'It was nothing,' Michael said, giving her an encouraging smile from where he lay on the ground. In truth, he ached in every bone of his body. It was only likely to get worse once the rush of the moment wore off and he could feel the injury in any real way.

He stared up the street, then shook his head in confusion, which made it hurt all the more. If he cared about the identity of the rider, or what had happened to the horse, he should be looking in the other direction.

Still, his eyes were drawn to the crowd that stood to the other side. Had there been a familiar face in it? Someone he recognised from another assignment, perhaps. He scanned the group and was overcome with the feeling that he was being watched. But that was ridiculous. The accident had made him the centre of attention. There was nothing unusual about a crowd gawping at him.

But this obvious explanation did not relieve the

prickling feeling at the back of his neck that someone was looking a little too intently.

'I have never been so frightened in my life,' Lady Olivia said, leaning over him and blocking his view.

This was doubtful, since she had been the one to find the murdered body of her father in her own home. But the idea that she was worrying about him was both flattering and distracting.

Now, she was helping him up out of the gutter where the galloping horse had left him with a blow from a hoof and a toss of his head. One hand held his, the other cradled his arm as she eased him to his feet.

He suppressed a groan. Now was not the time to sound less than heroic. It was also a comfort to know that he had managed to miss the worst of the refuse in the street. A bit of dust and a torn coat sleeve was nothing his pride could not recover from. 'I assure you I have borne worse. It was not pleasant, of course. But the important thing is that you were safely out of the way when it happened.'

The smile she gave him at this comment was enough to daze the strongest man. He could hardly be blamed for his reaction to it, which was to grin like a mooncalf.

'I think we both need to refresh ourselves. We can hire a carriage to take us for tea, and then home,' she said, eyeing his gait as if searching for a limp.

He wanted to argue that it was not necessary, he was fine to walk. But it would be a lie, for he was shaken to the bone. Fortunately, it was not really his place to tell her how this trip was to end. 'I will purchase you an ice, if you wish one,' he said, raising a hand to hail a cab.

'Mr Solomon, may I speak to you in the study, please?' The Duke was standing in the door at the back of the house, frowning at him expectantly.

He rose uneasily from the bench in the garden and tried not to limp as he walked towards the house. The incident with the horse on the previous day had gone better than it might have, in that he had taken only one kick to the arm that had knocked him back onto the pavement. Another step forward and he might have gained a split skull for his pains.

But he doubted that Scofield cared about his personal problems. Judging by the look on the man's face, he had done something to displease the peer. He could think of several things that qualified but had no intention of volunteering information that might get him dismissed...or worse.

He followed the Duke into the house and down the hall to the study, standing in front of a chair until Scofield closed the door behind him and gave him leave to sit. Then, with no further preamble, he announced, 'My sister was seen on Bond Street.' Then he added, 'With a man.'

'Oh,' he said, trying to decide how best to explain what had happened. 'That was me. She wished to go shopping. Since it would have been an excellent opportunity to meet with Clement, I accompanied her.'

'That does not explain why you were sitting in Gunter's, eating sorbet with her.'

'Technically, that is not true. I had a piece of sponge cake, and not a single bit of her sorbet.'

The Duke's expression—already ominous—turned darker still. 'When I hired you, your references said you were an ingenious man, Mr Solomon. They did not say that you were glib.' Then he fixed Michael with a stare to inform him that they were not speaking of a virtue.

'I try not to be, Your Grace.'

'I suggest you try harder,' he replied. 'Now, will you please explain to me what you were doing sitting at the same table with my sister, eating confections when you should have been working.'

'There was an accident,' he said, trying his best to diminish the event that had left him bruised and limping. 'A runaway horse.' He held up a hand in reassurance. 'You sister was in no way injured, but it did upset her. I escorted her to the tea shop, so she might calm her nerves before returning home.'

'My sister is not the nervous sort,' he said, still suspicious.

And yet she had been quite concerned when he'd been struck down in the street and had insisted that they go somewhere to sit until she was sure he had recovered. She had then plied him with cake and tea, asking him to tell her about his work, and assure her that he had been in situations much more dangerous than this.

Her attention had made him forget all about the feeling that they were being observed. But the Duke's detailed knowledge of their activities proved he had been right.

'I am waiting for an explanation, Mr Solomon.'

'It was a long morning for her. If she wanted a sorbet, I did not feel that it was my place to deny her. Nor did I want to leave the seat opposite her open, should the whole trip be a ploy to meet Clement.'

'About Clement,' Scofield said, eyes narrowed. 'You have stopped two attempts to elope already.'

Michael nodded, glad that the conversation had returned to his successes.

'The second attempt ended on the road to Gretna. But you knew about it when they were still in London.'

Again, Michael nodded.

'Why did you wait?' the Duke demanded. 'If you had failed, I might have lost my sister.'

'If I had stopped her too soon, she might have become even more strongly attached to the idea of elopement,' he replied. 'Hopes that are raised will dash all the harder when allowed a bit of height. As it was, a brief trip north with her supposed hero left her quite disappointed in the fellow. I suspect they will try again soon, and Clement's inability to carry out the planning will continue to disappoint her.'

'Or it could simply be a flair for the dramatic on your part,' Scofield said, frowning. 'In any case, keep it firmly in mind that if you allow them too much latitude and damage my sister's reputation, it will go as bad for you as it will for Clement.'

'Of course, Your Grace.'

'Likewise, if I hear any more fustian out of you about sponge cake and overwrought nerves, the loss of your position will be the least of your worries.'

'I understand,' Michael replied, burying his annoyance under a neutral smile. It appeared that the Duke was not satisfied with a single guard but had set someone to follow them on their trip to Bond Street. Or had they just been seen by some friend of his who'd recognised Lady Olivia?

The lack of confidence in his abilities was insulting. But it was even more annoying that the Duke was upset over a few minutes of innocent conversation in a tea shop. It made him seem as insane as his sister claimed he was.

'Let us hope so,' Scofield said, giving him a slow and considering look. 'And I hope that, in setting you to watch over my sister, my problems will cease, and not become worse.'

Michael frowned, confused.

The Duke gave him another pointed look. 'My sister is a most attractive young lady, and quite wilful. I do not know what lengths she might go to, should she truly want to escape the house.' Now, he was looking at Michael as if he were the sort of unplumbable depth that a proper lady might sink to if she had no other alternative.

'You think that yesterday she was trying to…' he

chose the next word with care '…co-opt me?' Because to suggest seduction was to admit that he had begun to think of her as something more than an assignment. In any case, he shook his head firmly. 'Once I have been set to a task I do not allow myself to be swayed from it by a sad story or a pretty face.' Especially when the story and face were attached to a woman whose social caste set her totally out of reach. Any ideas he'd had while with her were the stuff of fantasy.

'I am glad we understand each other,' Scofield said with a chilly smile. 'Because if you fail in that way, I will see to it that you never work for anyone ever again.' It was as if a mask had slipped and revealed the peer's true character. Though his expression displayed no hint of anger, there was something in the tone that implied an end far more permanent than a few bad references.

Michael suppressed a shudder, not wanting to seem anything less than completely confident in his own abilities. 'You have nothing to fear, Your Grace.'

Of course he didn't. It was those in proximity to him that needed to be afraid. The Duke gave a slight nod to indicate that their meeting was at an end, and Michael rose stiffly and returned to his place in the garden.

Mr Solomon had returned from her brother's study and was now sitting under his tree, looking very much as he always did. She could easily imagine what her brother had said, for he had quizzed her over breakfast to get the details of what had happened yesterday.

She had the distinct impression that he thought something had occurred between them other than a simple shopping trip.

She sighed. If it had, she would not have minded so very much. She supposed it made her shallow, to want to run away with Alister and still long for kisses from Mr Solomon. But yesterday he had been ready to use his own body to shield her from a wild horse. Add to that the compliments he had paid her and the kiss he had already given her, and she could not deny that she found him very attractive.

She was sure the feeling would fade if Alister would do his job and arrange another meeting. Of course, the last elopement had been rather disappointing, and not just because of its sudden ending. He might as well have gone out of his way to say things designed to make her cross. It was clear that he did not like her sister, or her dogs. After marriage, she might win him over on the idea of visits from Peg, but she suspected that her beloved pugs would be lost to her for ever.

There had to be some way to secure their future. Who did she know who was reasonable, responsible and kind enough to take care of them for her?

She walked through the kitchen, collecting the requisite scraps for the pugs and then out into the garden. She went first to the dogs, distributing their dinners and smiling down on them while they ate. 'It is all right, little ones,' she said. 'I think I have found the answer to our problem.' Then she strode down the garden walk towards Mr Solomon. The dogs looked up from the last of their food and followed her, intrigued.

She was standing in front of him now, waiting to catch his attention. He did not immediately look up when her shadow fell upon his face and she wondered if he was actually asleep and unable to hear her or whether, after his talk with her brother, he had decided it was in his best interests to ignore her.

She cleared her throat, forcing him to notice her. He started at the sound of her voice, and when he opened his eyes she said, 'May I ask a favour of you?' She balled her fists in her pockets so he would not see how tense she was.

He answered in the same careful tone he often used. 'As long as it does not interfere with the duties I have been hired to do, I see no reason why I could not help you.'

This sudden distance was her brother's fault then. Mr Solomon sounded much more interested in his duty than he had been yesterday, while carrying her hatbox. 'When I am gone...' she began.

He laughed. 'Are you languishing away after less than a month in my company? It is not that bad, is it?'

'I mean gone from this house,' she said, annoyed. 'When I have eloped with Alister.'

'That will not happen, if I have my way.'

'I am aware of your intent. But if I manage to get away despite that...' she began again. 'Would you take my dogs?'

He started again, then looked down at the dogs tugging on her skirts. 'You do not want to keep them?'

'I do,' she said quickly. 'But Alister said there will not be room for them. And no one in my brother's household likes Caesar.'

'He does not seem so bad to me,' Mr Solomon said, running his hand down the dog's back and causing his back legs to kick in euphoria.

'Now, perhaps,' she said. 'But Caesar was a very bad dog for a very long time. The staff is quite out of patience with him. And my brother...' She did not even want to think about that. 'He is not good with people, and I doubt he would be any better with animals should I make him angry.'

'I see.' Mr Solomon frowned. 'And Clement says there will be no room in your new home?'

'Despite what Alister thinks, they do not take up much space,' she said hurriedly, wondering if the house Mrs Solomon described had room for two small dogs. 'I would be happy to give you some of my allowance, if that would make it easier to afford.'

'That will not be necessary,' he said briskly. 'I am fully capable of paying the upkeep of these two. And, unlike some people, I will not claim that I lack the space for them, since I am not in the habit of lying to a woman I am fond of, just to avoid the responsibility of caring for their needs.'

'Alister is not lying,' she insisted, then stopped. Had he just admitted to being fond of her? But when she looked at him again there was no sign of excess emotion on his face. And Alister couldn't be lying. Even if he was, it was not such a big lie. He had probably only told it to avoid hurting her feelings.

It was painful to think he did not want her dogs any more than he had wanted her sister. Or was hurt even the right word? Perhaps it was a change of feeling that she feared.

Mr Solomon had noticed her silence and was staring at her expectantly. 'Have you visited the home of the man you intend to marry?' he asked. His tone was faintly annoyed, as if it disappointed him to find that she was so obtuse to what was happening around her.

'Of course not,' she snapped. 'My brother does not want me spending time with Alister at all, much less travelling to his property.'

'He has a nice set of rooms on Jermyn Street,' Mr Solomon supplied. 'And an estate with several acres in Lambeth, not far from the city.'

'How do you know these things?' she asked, surprised. It was more information than she had gathered from her suitor in the years they'd spent together.

'I make it a point of learning as much as I can about the people I am set to follow,' Solomon said, shrugging one shoulder. 'I find it is much easier to do my job when I am not constantly surprised by details.'

'Oh,' she said. It made sense, of course. But it also made her wonder what this man had learned about her. Not that there was anything to learn, other than that she was the sister of a duke. Other more personal details—her favourite colour, her favourite food, her hopes and dreams beyond marrying Alister—would not have been useful, or attainable. She had no real friends to confide in, nor did she often leave the house.

'Last year Clement inherited his house from an uncle,' Solomon added. 'A man of some means.'

'He is an orphan,' she supplied, glad to prove that she did not live in total ignorance. Then she frowned. She had always felt sorry for him and assumed that he needed her because he was alone in the world, poor and friendless. But it seemed that he'd had at least some family until recently. And Mr Solomon had said that the inheritance from his uncle was recent, but Alister had not mentioned it at all.

She had imagined constrained financial circumstances in their marriage and had prepared herself for it. They might struggle, but they would do it together. She had decided to view the downward change in her life as refreshing and exciting, rather than depressing. She had got no pleasure from being a member of a rich and powerful family. As long as they had love, life with an impoverished Alister would be better than that.

But now it seemed she had not understood at all. Why had Alister not explained to her that he had a home and a fortune? It seemed, even after all the time they had spent together, she knew very little about his actual life, beyond the fantasy that she'd created around him.

'You will not have to concern yourself about the

animals,' Mr Solomon said, bringing her back to reality. 'I have no intention of letting you run off with this man. And it is probably just as well, if he is not willing to take this charming creature.' He lifted his foot and, along with it, the dog that had sprawled over his boot, letting the limp pug flop back into the grass.

'He will come round in time, I am sure,' she said, imagining how easy it would be to hide Caesar and Cleo on several acres of a country estate.

'Even if he does not, I am sure you have no reason to worry. He and his mate have been thriving here and will continue to do so.' Now Cleo had found Mr Solomon's other boot and was worrying at the toe of it, her crooked fangs making equally uneven gouges in the leather. It surprised her that Mr Solomon seemed more amused than bothered. He was staring down at the dog with an indulgent smile.

She smiled as well, though still worried. 'The staff loathe him and would be glad to see him gone. He has been so much trouble for so long. And as I said before, I worry that my brother might act rashly, should I anger him.'

'Surely not!' Did Mr Solomon truly not understand who had hired him? He looked up to give her a direct stare. 'I do not think your brother is the sort to kick a dog in a fit of pique. It is far more likely that he will give me a good thrashing for letting you get away.'

She had not thought of that. There was a much more satisfying object to bear the brunt of Hugh's anger, should she finally escape. With the idea came an unpleasant foretaste of guilt. Mr Solomon's successes at thwarting her thus far had been annoying, but that did not mean she wanted him to be punished when she finally succeeded, any more than the dog. 'I trust you will be clever enough to stay clear of him, should I manage to best you.'

'I will, and you will not,' he said with a firm smile, shaking Cleo free from his boot and lifting her in the air for a pat.

She shrugged, then reached down to pet the other dog. 'All the same, Caesar is not well loved in this family. I would prefer that you took him, or at least one of the puppies that are likely to appear.'

Mr Solomon glanced at the thickening dog in his hand. 'Puppies?'

'Of course,' she said with a laugh. 'They cannot seem to leave each other alone. It is only since I have got Cleo to keep him company that Caesar has become the adorable animal you see here.' She smiled down at her pet. 'Love has changed him.'

Solomon laughed. 'Dogs do not fall in love.'

She blinked in surprise. 'This dog has.'

Mr Solomon gave her a pitying look. 'I am sorry to be the one to explain this to you, but the emotion he experienced is far more base and animalistic than you'd like to think.'

'I know my dog far better than you,' she said, giving

him her frostiest glare. 'And he loves Cleo as much or more than he ever loved me.'

He shook his head. 'You are attributing an emotion to the little fellow that I have yet to see in people, so I have my doubts.'

It was her turn to laugh. 'You speak as if you don't believe in love at all.'

'Why should I?' he said, giving her a blank look in return. 'I have never felt it.'

'Your mother obviously loves you,' she said, smiling.

'That is not the sort of love I am talking about,' he replied.

'She also seems to be quite the romantic,' she said.

'My mother is quick to talk of love in relation to a man who might be no more real than the rest of her stories. It appears that he got what he wanted from her and left.' He ticked off two of his fingers to demonstrate, then raised a third and fourth. 'I suspect you think yourself in love with Clement. But your eagerness to elope has more to do with escaping your brother than anything that gentleman offers.' Then he focused on her, his gaze travelling slowly up and down, making her shiver. 'It is clear what he sees in you, and it has nothing to do with love.'

Perhaps he was right. The touch of his eyes on her body raised something in her that had nothing to do with love as she understood it. Despite the fact, she wanted more of it, like some illicit drug shared in a den of sin. That was reason enough to deny it. She was sure, if she succumbed, this Mr Solomon would disappear afterwards, just as his father had.

She straightened and shook off his gaze with a full-bodied shudder of mock revulsion. 'That is what you think, is it? Proof enough that you should keep your opinions to yourself, Mr Solomon. Now, will you take a dog, or not?'

His eyes hardened. 'The day you marry Alister Clement, I will take all the dogs you have to offer and a clowder of cats as well. But that day will never come, so neither of us need worry about them.'

'It will come,' she insisted. 'Sooner than you think.' But, even as she spoke the words, the old panic was rising, making her wonder if what he said was true. Suppose she did not love Alister, and he did not love her? When she woke at night in the throes of a nightmare, she needed the reassurance that only a lover could offer. She needed someone full of hope, who would tell her that the past was the past and the future would be all right. And a man who would wait for years had hope in his heart, if nothing else.

But she did not know when or if she would see Alister again, and what he would say to her when she did. And if he did not love her, any words she might hear from Mr Solomon were not worth the breath it took to say them. She could not count on him to stay any longer than his father had.

'Alister loves me,' she said, as much to herself as to

him. 'We will get away from you. And when that happens, you will be sorry.' Then, before tears could overtake her, she hurried back to the house.

## Chapter Eight

That night, the dream came back again.

She was standing in the doorway of her father's study, ready to wish him goodnight. But he was already asleep, his head cradled in his folded arms on the desk. She laughed and told him he was silly to be here, when there was a warm drink and a soft bed waiting upstairs.

Then she came forward and reached to shake his shoulder. Instead, she felt the knife and the wetness spreading on his coat.

She screamed, or at least tried to. The only sound she could manage was an eerie whisper of what the real scream had been. That night, it had gone on and on and she could not seem to remember how it stopped. Suddenly she was back in her bed, frozen and unable to move, her mouth still open as she struggled for breath that would not come.

It ended in a gasp and she sat bolt upright, shaking. In the darkness, she reached out for someone before remembering that she was alone. When Peg was still in the house, she would sometimes creep down the hall and climb into bed with her, eased by her sighs and snores, happy to know that there was someone sleeping close by.

But Peg was gone, and she was alone. So she did the only thing she could and lay back down, closing her eyes tight and hugging herself, imagining the arms belonged to Alister, imagining the comforting words he would whisper in her ear to ease her back to sleep.

But tonight, instead of hearing Alister's voice in her head, she heard Michael Solomon. She felt his arms around her, stiff and awkward at first, then tightening to hold her and finally muttering, 'There, there,' as he had the last time he had stopped her elopement.

And, against all intentions, she fell back into peaceful sleep.

The next morning Michael chose to walk to his assignment, though it was nearly five miles from Cheapside to the Scofield townhouse. He needed something to clear his head from the difficult night's sleep gained after speaking with Lady Olivia in the garden.

He had doubted the Duke's objections towards Clement at first. But it seemed that the peer was not so much an overprotective brother as he was an astute judge of character. Clement was in no way worthy of the woman who had fallen in love with him.

Though he had never owned a pet of his own, he understood the affection that many owners had for them.

The idea that Clement would separate Olivia from the animals she was so fond of was anathema. It was clear that he had both the land and the money to take them in. But he had lied to her, allowing her to believe otherwise.

It made Michael wonder what other desires on the part of the lady would be viewed as inconveniences by her future husband. Granted, a man had rights, both legal and moral, to set what limits he chose on the behaviour of his spouse. But Michael had never understood the pathological need some men had to set boundaries.

If he were marrying such a woman, he would allow her to keep as many dogs as she wished. Of course, he had no intention of marrying, ever. Even if he did, it would not be to Lady Olivia Bethune, who would not have him, even if he asked.

But she did like him well enough to trust him with her dogs. It was an unexpected show of faith that made him feel strangely happy. Along with her childish optimism about love amongst the canine species, it was quite endearing.

Which made it all the more galling that she was wasting herself on Clement. If they married, he would have her firmly under his thumb in a way that was much more restrictive than anything she had known from her brother. And he would do it secure in the knowledge that it was his right as husband.

Michael's lip curled at the thought. It was the way of small men everywhere to make themselves feel larger by subjugating the women in their lives. No matter Scofield's motive in preventing the marriage, Michael had his own reason for helping. He would save Olivia, whether she wanted it or not.

But what was he saving her for? That was the question. Not for himself, surely. If he wished a woman, there were easier ways to get one than forming a permanent attachment. And even if he decided to marry, he would have to look far lower than the sister of a duke. His income was sufficient for keeping her in pug dogs, but not much else. And that did not even cover the fact that her brother would murder him before he got the offer fully out of his mouth.

'Excuse me, sir.' A stranger was approaching, and Michael gave an acknowledging nod and stepped to the side, assuming he wished more of the pavement to pass him by.

Instead, the fellow turned as they came abreast and walked along at his side.

It was odd. He'd have expected and guarded against such behaviour in a bad neighbourhood at night. But he did not expect it from a properly dressed gentleman walking in Mayfair. Other than his manners, there was nothing suspicious about the man now walking beside him. He was dressed in a smartly tailored coat and a gold watch chain spread across his waistcoat, hinting at both wealth and taste. Though Michael was sure he had never seen the man before, there was still something familiar about him that could not be placed.

'A fine day, isn't it?' the man began. He sounded faintly anxious, though the words were innocuous enough.

'Indeed,' Michael replied, still unsure of why they were speaking at all.

'You are Michael Solomon, are you not?'

'I am,' he said, annoyed. 'But I do not believe I know you, sir.'

The snub should have been enough to send him away. Instead, the man laughed nervously and continued to keep pace with him. 'Of course not. It has been a long time. Too long for you to remember me, I am sure. I am... I was...acquainted with your mother.'

The audacity of the man, to claim a connection in such a way. Michael picked up his pace and kept his eyes straight ahead. The Scofield townhouse was less than a quarter mile away and he could not have a complete stranger trailing him into the garden.

'I am aware that you live with Maria in Gracechurch Street, and am eager to pay her a visit.'

Michael snorted. 'Do you wish my permission to do so? If you are a friend of such old standing, I think she can decide for herself.'

'I was hoping that you would tell me the number,' he said, then waited expectantly.

'Certainly not,' Michael replied. 'If you do not know her direction, you will not have it from me.'

The man stopped short, and when Michael continued to walk, called after him, 'Have you not realised who I am?'

'No,' Michael called back over his shoulder. 'Nor do I wish to know. Good day to you, sir.'

He hurried down the street, trying to shake the uneasy feeling that the man had raised in him. After the interview in the Duke's study, he suspected Scofield was spying on him. But it made no sense to send someone who would ask after his mother. If the man truly was an acquaintance of hers, Michael could not remember ever seeing him, nor had his mother announced that she was expecting company.

He arrived at the Scofield townhouse a short time later, only to find the place in an uproar. The butler rushed up to him when he was barely through the gate. 'It is Lady Olivia, Mr Solomon. She has been taken!'

Michael calmed the man enough to get the full story from him, not that there was much to tell. The night guard had already gone, and he had not yet arrived. Lady Olivia had been feeding her dogs when a masked man appeared and grabbed her, covering her head with a cloth bag before rushing her to a waiting carriage and driving away. Further questioning revealed that the man was about the right height to be Alister Clement, and the carriage was a yellow post-chaise, missing paint on the left rear wheel.

The incident was his fault, for taking the time to walk. If he had been here, he might have stopped the trouble before it started, as the Duke wished him to.

Now he would have to hurry to catch them up. He called for a horse from the Duke's stable and headed for the north road, praying that Clement had not decided to get inventive in his navigation.

In the carriage, Liv struggled free of the cloth over her face and the panic that accompanied it. It was some slight relief to see Alister in the seat beside her, beaming in triumph. But it hardly made up for her racing pulse, and the fear that her brother had finally gone mad and she was about to end up like her father.

'You needn't have grabbed me,' she said, rubbing feeling back into her arms and wrapping them around her body to stop the trembling. 'I'd have come with you willingly if you had just asked.'

'I wanted it to be spontaneous,' he said, still smiling and oblivious to how badly he had frightened her. 'Solomon has been able to keep up with us so far. But this time he will have had no chance to ascertain the time of our departure.' There was a certain accusatory tone to this statement that she did not appreciate.

'He was not getting the information from me, if that is what you are thinking,' she said, annoyed. 'The first time he guessed, and the second time he found your note.'

'And today there was no time for you to prepare,' he said. 'And no time for him to be ready either.'

That meant that she had left her meagre possessions behind. She remembered the day her sister had run off with Mr Castell with nothing but the clothes on her back. There was no evidence that she regretted the act. Her bedroom was just as it had been when she had left. As far as Liv knew, she'd made no effort to call for anything she'd forgotten.

Of course, she did not have dogs. And she had left a sister behind to take care of anything important that had been forgotten.

But Alister was probably right. This time, since there had been no warning at all, it was unlikely that Mr Solomon would be able to catch up with them. Why then was this not making her happier? The fact that she would not see that man again should make her light-headed with freedom. Instead, it seemed like another loss. Perhaps there would be some way she could find him later to say goodbye.

And then she remembered he had promised to take all of her dogs, and a clowder of cats, should she manage to best him. She was not even sure how many animals that might entail, but she sincerely hoped that it was many and that they were very troublesome. The mental image of moggies on the chairs and tables, snoozing on sofas and walking back and forth on the pianoforte had her smiling again.

'See? As I told you, it will all be better now,' Alister said, mistaking the reason for her changed mood.

'Of course,' she said, forcing her enthusiasm to turn to the day ahead. Then she thought of what Michael had told her about Alister's holdings and the possibility that she could keep her dogs, after all. 'Alister, when we are done in Scotland, will we be living on your uncle's estate, or will we take a house in London?'

He frowned. 'What do you know of my uncle, or his estate?'

'Michael Solomon told me that you inherited…'

'Debt,' he said, cutting her off before she could finish. 'I inherited my uncle's debts along with his land. If you think that I can keep you in a fancy house, as your brother did, you are sorely mistaken.'

'That is not it at all,' she said, eager to make amends. 'It is just that you never mentioned you had an uncle. I assumed you were alone in the world.'

'Because we were estranged,' he replied. 'I did not expect an inheritance from him, nor do I know what to do with the problems he has left me.'

'I am sorry,' she said quickly. 'I did not understand.'

'No, you did not,' he snapped.

'But now I do,' she said, trying to smile. 'It is just that I had hoped, if you had troubles you would share them with me.'

'What good would that do?' he asked, puzzled.

She did not know. But she had hoped that he would derive some of the comfort from her that she'd hoped to gain from him.

'It is up to me to solve your problems,' he said, patting her hand. 'You cannot be expected to solve mine.'

Her smile faded again, and she stared out through the back window towards the townhouse that was

already out of sight and wondered if that were true. She
had hoped that just being with Alister would be enough
to take away her fears, but she did not feel the grip of
them lessening in any way. Would she have to spend
the entirety of her life tossing and turning at night and
looking back over her shoulder during the day, in fear
of seeing her brother and in hope of seeing Michael
Solomon?

Her sister had managed to escape the past, or she
seemed to have. She realised she had only Hugh's word
that Peg and her husband were still alive. Until she had
spoken to her, touched her, seen her, Liv would not believe that her sister was all right.

'I was wondering,' she said, hesitating, 'if you had
considered my request to visit my sister.'

'Reconsidered, you mean,' he said, staring out of the
window. 'Why is this so important to you?'

'Because…she is my sister,' Liv said, wondering if it
was because Alister had no siblings that he found this
so hard to understand. 'I have not seen her since she
ran away. It has been almost six months.'

'Then you should be growing used to her absence,'
he said, as if this should settle the matter.

'On the contrary, I miss her more each day,' she replied.

'But that does not change the fact that the wife of a
tattler for a scandal sheet is not the sort of company I
would wish a wife of mine to associate with,' Alister
said with a shake of his head.

'We cannot avoid association,' she said. 'She is my family.'

'She was your family,' he said firmly. 'As of today, I am your family. You do not need your sister, or your brother, with his dubious reputation. From now on, you will have me, and that is all you will need.'

For a moment she could not breathe. She had escaped her brother's house and nothing had changed. She would just be living in another man's house instead. And, though he was not a murderer, Alister seemed to be under the impression that she did not need any more company than his own, and needed no more freedom than he was willing to allow her.

She wanted to shout to the driver to stop the coach. She wanted to get out, to run through the fields beside the road until she was clear of all of mankind, to hide in the grass like a rabbit, still and scared, until everyone tired of looking for her.

Then she remembered that there was someone who would never tire until he had found her. 'What will we do if Mr Solomon catches us again?' she said, in hope rather than fear.

'Then we will elope again,' Alister said, relaxing into the seat. 'We will run away as many times as are necessary until we succeed, and he and your brother will admit defeat.'

'Oh,' she said. The man who had waited for her for two years and more was clearly the man who could wait out the opposition, fomenting plot after plot until he got them to Gretna. There was nothing particularly romantic about a war of attrition, but it seemed that that was what they were fighting. She could not exactly complain about it. It was the future she had been hoping for. Now that it was here, it was too late to request a change of plan.

They rode for several hours until the sun was low on the horizon and the clear day had clouded to a promise of a stormy evening. The first raindrops were falling when they reached the inn where Alister said they would stop for the night. It was further than they had got on their last aborted escape, and she was torn between hope and despair. Some part of her had been assuming that Mr Solomon would stop them in the middle of the road, as he had the last time.

But he had not arrived. And if Alister chose to take advantage of their first night alone to show her he loved her in the most physical way possible, she could not refuse him. She had been anticipating this night for as long as she could remember. Her sister had assured her that, if it was done in love, there was nothing wrong with it.

But now that the moment was near, she wondered if that was the truth of her heart. She could not believe that love did not exist, as Mr Solomon claimed. She had only to remember the look in Peg's eyes as she had talked of David Castell. But suppose Mr Solomon was right that she did not love Alister? None of what had happened today resembled the secure and happy future she had been hoping for.

It did not matter. Perhaps a deepening of feeling was something that came with intimacy. And they would be married in another day or two. It would be better than the life she had, because she would find a way to make it so. As Alister led her into the taproom of the inn, she worked hard to clear her mind of all negative thoughts. It was just the two of them. No one would be arriving to interrupt. Nothing would be prevented.

Or spoiled. She meant spoiled. At least she was sure that Alister loved her. He would not have gone to all this trouble otherwise. He gave her an encouraging smile as he left her in the corner and enquired about dinner and the finest room for him and his wife.

A single room, then. That answered the question of intimacy. She felt her heart give another nervous flutter.

'Not a room to be had,' the innkeeper said with a smile.

'I beg your pardon?' Alister was staring at him as if the possibility was not one he had considered.

'We have coach passengers planning to spend the night on the benches of the coffee room,' the innkeeper said, beaming at the success he was having. 'There is some space left, of course.'

'We will take the room,' Alister said quickly.

'I said space. The room itself is not exactly empty,' the innkeeper went on.

'I beg your pardon?' Alister said again, still confused.

'The room is large, warm and dry. I might be able to persuade its occupant to share the mattress. And I believe there is a chair...'

'Devil's teeth,' said Alister, thoroughly undone. 'I am travelling with a lady.'

'It is that or the coffee room,' the innkeeper insisted. 'Your wife will not be at risk as long as you are there to protect her.'

'Lead us to it then,' her companion said through gritted teeth. Then he muttered to her, 'I will see if money can persuade the fellow to budge so we might have some privacy.'

'That is not necessary,' she whispered, afraid to tell him that the romantic mood, if ever there had been one, was ruined. With the inn packed to the rafters, she did not imagine there would be much privacy, even if they emptied the room. And the presence of a chaperone, however unwanted, would give her one more night before the inevitable.

She climbed the stairs behind Alister and the innkeeper, her head hung, hoping that if she did not see the people around her, perhaps they would not notice her either and she might pretend that this night had not happened at all.

They reached the top of the stairs and the innkeeper led them to the left, past several doors before rapping smartly on the panels of one halfway down the corridor. 'Mr Solomon, I must ask for your indulgence.'

*Dear God, no.*

When the door opened her worst nightmare stood framed in the doorway, stripped to his shirtsleeves and beaming at them as if he had been expecting them all along. Knowing him, he probably had. 'Welcome, friends. It is a dashed bitter night out there. But there is a stove here, the sheets are clean and the mattress tight. I am sure we shall all be cosy.'

'We most certainly will not,' Alister said, fists balled. 'The lady and I will set out for Scotland on the first coach available.'

'There is a driving rain, which I did not orchestrate,' Mr Solomon said with a smile, 'although it is quite convenient. One might even take it as an omen from the Almighty.'

'In the morning, then,' Alister said. 'After a night in the coffee room.'

'For you, perhaps. But the lady with you is so exhausted she is swaying on her feet. She will stay in this room with me.'

'And what makes you think you are worthy of her company, unescorted in the small hours?'

'Of the two of us, I assume her brother would prefer it to be me rather than you,' Solomon said, looking him up and down in challenge. 'But if you do not trust me, then the three of us will stay here together. I have already arranged for the return trip to London on the morrow. You will find that the coachman who brought you thus far will not be willing to risk going against the Duke of Scofield to take you one foot further up the road.'

Alister looked from Michael to her and back again, then seemed to relent. 'Very well, then. We will share the room. We shall take the bed, and you the floor.'

At this, Michael laughed. 'Do you think I will let you make mischief under the blankets?' He pointed to the mattress. 'It is wide enough for three.' Then he threw himself on top of the covers in the middle of it and patted either side.

'You don't honestly suggest…?' Alister said.

'I do not suggest,' he said with an icy smile. 'I insist. You can take off your boots and help yourself to the side near the door. And, should you get up in the night, I don't care if you need to leave to go to the privy or to perdition, as long as you go alone.'

Then he glanced at Liv. 'You, my lady, shall take the side closest to the fire, and the extra pillow as well. There is a screen in the corner, should you wish to loosen your stays. I will turn my back for privacy and will remain here, between you.' Now his grin was positively devilish. 'Blow out the candle when you are ready, Clement. Tomorrow is a busy day. We cannot stay up all night.'

'You are out of your mind,' Alister said, staring at him.

'I should think you are the crazy one, if you wish

to take the lady away from her loving and homicidal brother,' Michael said, still smiling. 'I, for one, plan to report to him that absolutely nothing happened this evening, which will assure the three of us that we will all be alive to greet the next week.' Finished speaking, he did as he had promised and turned away from her so she could prepare for bed.

She did little more than remove her shoes and climb under the covers, since the situation was far too strange to consider undressing. Once she had claimed her spot, he shifted until his body rested against hers, hard as a rock wall on the other side of the blankets.

Alister groaned and she felt the ropes creak as he took his place on the other side.

'You will pay for this, Solomon,' Alister muttered.

'Be paid a bonus, more likely,' the man next to her said. 'Now shut your gob and let us try to get some sleep.'

Alister snuffed the candle and the room was reduced to gloom from the lit coach yard outside the window and the flickering light from the window of the stove.

Liv lay as still as she could, staring at the ceiling, surprised to find that she was suppressing a giggle. The situation was ludicrous and completely unexpected.

Perhaps not completely. In her heart, she had known that Mr Solomon would put a stop to the elopement before anything happened. He was too clever to be beaten. But she had not imagined that she would end the night sleeping beside him. She glanced in his direction and, as if he sensed it, he rolled onto his side to face her.

His eyes were closed as if he slept, or feigned it, but his lips were curled in a satisfied smile, as if he knew she watched him and shared her sense of the absurd. His eyelashes were gold-tipped by the banked fire in the stove and the shadows bounced off the planes of his face, accentuating the high cheekbones and the firm chin.

If she had seen him like this in the garden, she'd have run for her sketch pad to draw him with strong, masculine swipes of her pencil, wanting to capture the memory so she might look at it again, when she was alone.

Suddenly, his eyes opened and he stared back at her, his gaze moving slowly down to her lips as if he was trying to memorise her face as she was his. She could feel it, like a fingertip tracing over her skin.

He was aware of what he was doing to her, she was sure. His smile had changed to something hungry, and his eyes dropped again, kissing her throat and caressing the swell of her breasts, though his body was still. Not a muscle moved to indicate what was happening between them.

But she could not seem to stay still. She arched her neck, offering herself to him and closing her eyes. Then she allowed her imagination to run free. In her mind, his hands went where his eyes had, stroking her skin, his mouth teasing her breasts. She tried to keep her breathing low and slow, like a sleeper in a dream. But the more

she imagined what he could do to her, the harder it was
to stay calm. She took a thin, hissing breath through her
teeth, only to exhale in a shudder that seemed to rock
her body to her toes.

When it happened again on the next breath, she could
see a spark of amusement in the dark blue eyes only a
few inches from hers, and she watched his lips part and
his tongue run along the inside of his teeth, as if considering which part of her to bite.

There was a strange, urgent heat rising in her. Her
legs felt restless and her body trembled. And then he
blinked, and she hiccuped and let out a final sigh as
the feeling dissipated as quickly as it had come.

He was grinning now, satisfied with what he had
done to her without even trying. It was probably why
he did not notice Alister shifting on the other side of
the bed.

Liv closed her eyes to slits, not wanting to be caught
awake, should he sit up to check on her. But he did not
seem interested in her at all.

She watched as his hand edged towards the heavy
pewter candlestick on the nightstand. Then, inch by
inch, he raised it high in preparation to roll his body
and bring it down on their chaperone's head.

Before she could manage to cry out a warning, Mr
Solomon saw the message in her eyes and rolled to face
the other side of the bed, one arm up to block the downward progress of the candlestick. The jolt of bone hit-
ting bone shocked the thing out of Alister's grasp and

it fell harmlessly on the bed as he snatched his arm back with a curse.

Mr Solomon retrieved the candlestick, muttering an apology as he reached over her to place it on the opposite nightstand, safely out of Alister's reach. Then he settled back to sleep, this time facing the door.

After a sleepless night, Mr Solomon followed them down to the coffee room, looking fresh and rested. He pulled a coin from his purse, waved it at a passing stable boy and enquired about the next coach for London. He bought two seats and looked expectantly at Alister. 'If you care to make it three I will not object, but neither will I pay for you. If you are not interested in that, the horse I hired to get me this far is waiting to be ridden back.' He grinned at Liv and explained, 'A man on horseback can travel faster than a coach, even when the coach has a head start of several minutes.' Then he ordered a hearty breakfast and settled himself on the nearest bench to wait.

Once he was a step or two away, Alister pulled her into a corner and said, 'You are not seriously going back with him, are you?'

'What choice do I have?' she said, feeling strangely relieved that it was all over.

'We can ignore him and walk out through the door right now. We can get on the next mail coach heading north. I can find our driver from yesterday and offer a bribe bigger than the one Solomon offered, and we can continue on our journey.'

'And he will come with us,' she said with a sigh. 'He will dog our every step until I agree to come back with him. He might push you into another ditch, for all I know. Or offer to witness the ceremony and then climb into our bed for the wedding night. Whatever he does, I doubt he will relent. All we can do is return to London and try another day.'

'If you are serious about marrying me, you will follow where I go,' he reminded her. 'But apparently you have no faith in my abilities.' The tone of the last sounded rather like pouting.

'I have faith in you,' she said quickly. 'But I also know when it is time to admit that we have lost a game, but not the match.'

'We cannot just give up,' he insisted.

'We are not giving up,' she said, trying to remain calm. 'We have waited this long. A little longer will do no harm.'

'You may go back with him if you like,' he snapped. 'I have no intention of riding in any coach he is taking.'

'Then you will be leaving me alone and unchaperoned with him,' she reminded him, as gently as possible.

'You shared a bed with the man last night,' Alister said, loudly enough to cause a lady in the tap room to eye them curiously.

'I shared a bed with both of you, and you know it was innocent,' she snapped back. 'But I would prefer that you not chide me over something that was none of my doing.'

'It was none of mine either,' he almost shouted. 'It was all that damned Solomon's fault.'

'He is only doing his job,' she said, realising immediately that it was the wrong thing to say if she wanted to calm him so that the other passengers would stop staring.

'Now, you are defending him,' Alister shouted. This time, she was sure it was a shout, for she could not remember ever hearing him this angry. 'It is as if you want him to succeed.'

'I do not,' she insisted. What she actually wanted was for her fiancé to not be so easily bested by him. That might be even worse, since she might be stuck with Alister, and his plans for her future. But if they were to part, she did not want to do it here, in front of a fascinated audience. 'But I am not so foolish that I do not recognise when he has succeeded. There is nothing to be done today, other than to go back to London.'

'Very well, then. Go!' he shouted. 'And we will see if I visit you again.'

It seemed, as in everything else, he was not leaving her the right to cast him off, as a gentleman should. He was intent on humiliating her. But, before she could respond again, Mr Solomon was there, wearing the same bland smile he always did when pretending to be professional.

'The coach is ready, Lady Olivia.' He glanced at Alister. 'Will you be accompanying us, Mr Clement?' Then he gave the man a look that said he had better not be.

'I am quite capable of finding my own way back,' Alister snapped, still staring at her as if he expected her to come away with him. Why did he think threats and shouting would have changed her mind?

She sighed, then glanced at Mr Solomon. 'I am ready.' She followed him out into the coach yard, head hanging in what she hoped looked like resignation.

If Alister was sincere and did not want her any more, it said very little in favour of continuing to ride with him. Nor did she want to be trapped in a carriage with him while he was still fuming. It was not her fault that things had worked out the way they had, and this time she was not going to take the blame for it.

Michael helped Lady Olivia up into her seat on the mail coach, then hopped in after her, looking across the body of the coach to where she was seated and wondering if she had ever taken such humble transport before. He thought not, for she was staring, fascinated, at the two other people sharing the seats, a sleepy vicar on her left and a farmer's wife on his right. Her eyes slid to him, then back to the ground in embarrassment.

If she was thinking of her response to him on the previous night, then she had reason to blush. He had never been with a woman so responsive that she could be brought to climax by an inquisitive look. If he had known what she was like, he would not have spent the

night on top of the covers like a nervous bride. He'd
have pushed Clement out through the door and escorted
her the rest of the way to Gretna.

It was a foolish thought, for he was likely to end up
bleeding into the Thames should he carry it out. The
innocent activities of last night would be hard enough
to explain to the Duke when they returned this afternoon. But, barring anything that might have happened
in the carriage on the way to the inn, he was returning
his charge undamaged.

The thought occurred to him that her amenable nature in bed might have been the end result of love play
with Clement. It might have had nothing to do with any
interest in his own person. Considering the audience
in the carriage today, they would not be exploring the
question while travelling. After hearing the argument
in the coffee room, the other two passengers would
push him out onto the road before letting him lay a
hand on her.

She looked at him now, her expression jaded. 'I hope
you are not going to gloat,' she said with a sigh. 'I do
not think I could bear it.'

'I see no reason to rub salt in the wounds,' he said
with a sympathetic smile. 'It has been a difficult enough
morning for you, without me adding to your unhappiness.'

'Do you think he is sincere in crying off?' she asked.

'It would make my job easier,' he admitted. 'But I
suspect it was an idle threat. Last night, he was ready

to brain me with a candlestick. That seems the action of a man committed to a course of action.'

'You knew,' she said, obviously surprised.

'It is what I would have done had someone played the despicable trick on me that I played on him,' he replied. 'In another life, he would have more of my sympathy.'

'If you ask me, you should consider it a blessing that he said he wanted no more of you. Bar the door to him the next time he comes round.' This comment came from the farmer's wife, who had been following the conversation with interest.

Michael tried not to smile as he watched the emotions flicker across Lady Olivia's face. First came the desire for the cut direct. Then for an announcement that she had not, in fact, asked for this woman's opinion. But, surprisingly, she just gave a nod of surrender.

Her acquiescence gave the vicar permission to contribute. 'I agree. If he is the sort to raise a candlestick in anger against another man, he will likely raise his hand to you, once you are married.'

The farmer's wife nodded enthusiastically.

In response, Lady Olivia looked baffled. 'He has never shown anything but kindness to me, and I have known him for years.'

'Of course not,' the farmer's wife said. 'Men are often different before they marry you. The ones that are the most difficult are the best at concealing it, or why would any woman have them?'

Olivia's eyes widened in response, and she leaned

forward to listen to more of the older woman's advice. Soon, she was peppering the other two with questions about her problem, and then with questions about their own lives, conversing with them as if they were old friends and not rude strangers.

Michael held his breath and his tongue, quietly amazed. If it had been any other lady of rank as august as hers, she'd have snubbed these people and lectured him for forcing her to endure their company. Instead, she was as polite and open to them as she would have been to her equals. Was she so starved for company? Or was she really as sweet-natured as she seemed to be?

He remembered the afternoon spent over the chess table, and the hour spent at Gunter's, and the playful way she'd spoken with his mother, who had been appallingly rude to her. He was wrong to have doubted her. Any other girl would have been haughty and difficult. But not his Olivia.

It was enough to give a man hope. He did not need it or want it, of course. She was the sort who deserved a husband, and he was never planning to be one of those. He would not risk bringing children into the world and forcing them to struggle as hard as he had to make a comfortable life. His income might stretch to cover a wife and her dogs, but there would never be enough to launch daughters and leave an inheritance to sons.

But, on a day like this, a little fantasy would do no

harm. Michael leaned back with a smile and tipped his hat over his eyes in preparation for a well-deserved nap and dreams of the fair Olivia.

## Chapter Nine

Michael went back to his house in Gracechurch Street, content with the way the day had gone. A pensive Olivia had been returned to her brother, who seemed surprisingly unconcerned with the damage to her honour that an overnight journey might have caused.

He had announced, 'When and if the time comes for her to marry, that will be the least of our worries.'

It had been a bizarre statement. But then, much of the behaviour of the peerage made no sense, and Scofield was the rule rather than the exception.

When it came to Olivia, it seemed that the words of the people in the carriage with them had done more to change her opinion of Clement than anything Michael and her brother had managed. Of course, foolish Alister had done much to dig his own grave by making a scene at the inn. Any sane man knew that you did not waste breath shouting at a woman, especially one that you had no legal hold over.

Once Lady Olivia was free of Clement, his job was

finished. If she was content to stay in her brother's house, a guard was not needed. It should not be surprising for he had known from the first this was a temporary position. It would end, as all his other assignments had. Then he would move onto the next one.

But what if he did not want to go? One simply did not tell one's employer—especially when that man was a duke—that one was not ready to leave. Nor could he announce that he had unfinished business with the lady, after an interesting interlude sharing a bed in an inn. She was a virgin, or at least pretended to be so. A twinkle in her eye and a quickening of body and breath did not give him the right to take anything more than his leave.

It was a relief to be back in his own home, where he knew his place and could try to free himself of foolish ideas about running back to Scofield House and declaring himself to Olivia. But, as he hung his hat on the hook by the door, he was surprised to see another man's hat on the side table, beside a pair of fine leather gloves.

He walked towards the sitting room and the sound of voices and laughter.

'Mother?' When he entered the room he was surprised yet again to see her hurriedly resuming her seat at the end of the couch, smoothing her gown and blushing as if he had interrupted something that she did not want him to see. 'What the devil?' It was the same fellow who had accosted him on the street yesterday.

'Language,' his mother said in response, smiling and shaking her finger at him.

'I think it is warranted,' he said, narrowing his eyes and glaring at the man sitting beside her.

'You will never guess what has happened,' his mother said, slapping her knees. 'Never in a million years.'

'Then why not tell me?' he replied, as exasperated with her as he always was.

'I am surprised that you have not guessed it already,' said the man, not bothering to introduce himself. 'But if you wish a clue, you might look in the mirror.'

He stared at the man, who had seemed familiar even though he was a stranger.

And then his mother laughed. 'It is your father, you silly boy. Mr Solomon.'

'There is no John Solomon,' Michael said, refusing to believe the truth that seemed to be before him.

'That is news to me,' the man said, patting the front of his coat as if assuring himself of substance. 'For I have known him now these fifty-six years.'

His mother laughed again. 'He means that he thinks you dead.'

That was not what he'd meant at all. The man was a figment of his mother's imagination, a falsehood that retained her reputation and kept him from being a bastard.

'Obviously, I am not dead,' the man assured him. 'And I have already assured your dear mother that I never meant to leave her. No thanks to His Majesty's Navy for press ganging me into service.'

'You have been in the navy all this time?' Michael said, sceptical.

'Not all,' the man admitted with a shrug. 'I was able to get away after seven years of service.'

'And once you did, you made no effort to contact this woman that you supposedly loved,' he countered.

'By the time he was able to post a letter, I had moved and left no forwarding direction,' she admitted. 'My family was not sympathetic to my condition, nor did they acknowledge our marriage. They would not allow me to come home, nor would they tell John where I had gone.'

'And how do you even know this man is the same one who left you?' Michael said, stabbing a finger in his direction. 'The whole idea is ludicrous. Appearing after thirty years. What does he want from you?'

'I do not want a thing from her,' the man said. Then he fished in his pocket. 'And perhaps this will go some way to assuring you of my identity. It is a miniature that your mother sat for, the year we met.' He pulled a tiny ivory oval from his pocket and passed it to Michael.

His mother leaned in from the other side. 'And do not dare say that it cannot be me, dear boy. I was young and beautiful once, not that you are likely to remember such a time. I sat for that painting the year of my come out and gave it to your father when he made his offer.'

'But what of the money that you have been receiving?' Michael asked. 'Where did that come from?' He had always imagined them to be discreet payments from the solicitor of a man who did not want to be named.

'I received a legacy from my family, as long as I promised to have no contact with them,' she admitted sadly. 'It was not a point of pride that my own parents were so scandalised by my elopement that they wanted no part in my life, or yours. But they sent me enough to live on and saw that you were educated, and that was something.'

'And you—' he turned back to the man who claimed to be his father '—where were you when not in the navy?'

'India,' he said with a smile, pulling out his watch fob and displaying the enormous ruby set in the end. 'There were many opportunities for a man of vision in that country, and I availed myself of all I could.'

'And you just decided to return now?' he said, still suspicious.

'Because the agents I had working for me in London had finally located your mother,' the man replied, turning to his wife with a fond smile. 'And, to my amazement, she has waited for me, just as I waited for her.'

'So you did not need me to give you this address,' he said, eyes narrowing.

'Not really,' the other man admitted. 'But it would have been nice had you offered it.'

'She thought you were dead,' Michael said, still not

sure what he was expected to feel at the presence of this interloper.

'Well, I am not. And the first thing I mean to do is get her out of these widow's weeds,' he said, grinning in triumph. 'We shall go to Bond Street, if that is still fashionable. We shall find you the best modiste that money can buy, and fit you out as you should be dressed, in all the colours of the season.' Then he reached into his pocket and withdrew a handkerchief, unknotting it to reveal a pair of ruby ear drops as big as any Michael had seen on the wives of the men he had worked for. 'A trip to the jeweller will be necessary later, but only to set the other stones I have brought back for you.'

His mother clasped her hands in front of her, enraptured, then leaned forward and threw her arms around the man who Michael still thought of as a stranger, not that it seemed to matter what he felt.

It was clear that she knew him well enough. She looked past the ear drops to the man who held them. 'They are beautiful, John. But all I needed was your return. I swear I feel ten years younger.'

And, hard as it was for Michael to admit, she was right. She was blushing like a schoolgirl, with a light in her eyes that had not been there for as long as he could remember.

'And soon we must sit down together, you and I, and work out the details of your inheritance,' John Solomon said, looking at Michael.

'I need nothing from you,' he blurted, confused. It

had been years since he had given up wishing for a father. And now here was a man trying to fill an empty slot that no longer existed.

'It is not a matter of need, dear boy. I am pleased that you have managed for yourself in my absence,' Solomon said, looking at him with unexpected paternal pride. 'But you should never have been forced to care for your mother. That was my job. And, while I thank you for doing it, I cannot let the matter go without making reparation.'

'You mean to pay me for doing my duty?' Michael said, indignant.

'I mean to give you a portion of your inheritance, more like,' he replied, smiling again. 'I am a very wealthy man, Michael. And so will you be, once I am gone, in truth.'

Michael could not manage any comment to this. Apparently, he was now rich. It was not that he did not want to be. But he did not want it to be the result of meeting this sham, who he'd been so sure did not exist. He backed slowly towards the door.

Solomon smiled at him. 'It is a lot to take in, is it not? Do not worry. We have all the time in the world to sort things out, now that I have found you and your mother again.'

'On the contrary,' Michael said. 'It has nothing to do with me at all. I am pleased that you have found each other, since it was clearly what you wanted. But do not involve me in your schemes for a happy family. I want no part of it.'

'Michael!' his mother said, clearly shocked.

The single word cut to his heart, just as it always did when he had done something to hurt or disappoint her. How could he? They were all to each other. She had been his protection and support when he was a child, and now, as an adult, he returned the duty. Except now she did not need him.

And he did not need the man at her side.

Without another word, Michael turned and left.

He walked the streets for a time, his mind reeling. Why had he left, when it was they who should be moving? He had bought the house with his own money, earned by honest labour. Said house could have but one master, and it would not be John Solomon.

Of course, with the house empty, he could easily fill it. The presence of his mother had not exactly prevented the idea, but it had given him an excuse to indulge his natural inclination, which was not to marry. In his opinion, such a union was not necessary for one who had no title to pass or estate to leave. It certainly was not something to be done in the name of love. One had only to look at his mother…

At least until today. Today, she had proved herself right and his own opinions—not quite wrong, exactly. What was the word he searched for?

Moot. His opinion on the subject of love was still

valid. It was still the last defence of the misguided and it was not something that could be ascribed to him. But the argument did not hold in the case of Maria Solomon.

He could marry, if only to find a way to dispose of his property on death. And if John Solomon insisted on foisting an inheritance on him, he could even marry Lady Olivia Bethune if he wanted to.

He froze.

Without thinking, he had walked all the way to the gate of the Scofield garden. It was night and not daytime, and there was no reason for him to be there. The household was settling down for the night, the doors were barred. He had even sent home the nightwatchmen he'd posted to take his place when he was not in the garden, as he'd deemed it unlikely that the girl would scarper back towards Scotland after the exhausting trip she'd just had.

He was alone, in a place he should not be, staring up at a house he did not belong in.

Then *she* appeared in an upstairs window. It must be her bedroom, for she had stripped to her shift, obviously getting ready for bed. The air was heavy with the fragrance of the wisteria climbing the back of the house, and her breasts rose and fell as she took in the scent.

His mouth went dry. It was lust. Nothing more than that. The night spent at her side had left him hungry for a woman. And the idea that he might use his newfound wealth, an inheritance he meant to refuse, to gain entrée to the upper classes so he might offer for her? His mind had sought an example of the most unattainable woman he could think of. It was nothing more than that.

And yet here he stood, wishing that the glowing fire that lit her room would render the thin cloth of her shift transparent. Or, perhaps, thinking she was alone, she might pull it off to let the moonlight touch her skin. She would glow like a pearl, he was sure, the warm palest pink, her breasts rose-tipped opal.

His palms cupped, he forced his hands into fists to avoid reaching for her, arms raised like a supplicant. Then a voice whispered softly from behind him. 'Stay away from her.'

He turned, shocked, to find a woman, heavily cloaked, standing a few feet off, staring at the house as he had done.

'I beg your pardon?' he said.

'Stay away,' she repeated. 'There is nothing but un-happiness for you if you involve yourself with her, or anyone else in the house. Leave before it is too late.'

Then she followed her own advice and hurried down the walk, leaving him too shocked to follow.

## *Chapter Ten*

She was falling in love with Michael Solomon.

Liv was not positive that this was the case. But, much as she might when catching a cold, she catalogued the symptoms and made a judgement from the result.

She had been stargazing out of the window last night, sighing in the moonlight in a way she had not done since Alister's first proposal. On the obverse, she should have been crushed by the things Alister had shouted at her in the taproom. Instead, she had been relieved. Relieved and a little excited to be taking a long coach ride with the man who had taken her away from her supposed beloved.

They had said very little to each other for the duration of the trip, but it had not mattered. She had been happy just to be with him, even if they were not alone. They had not been alone in the inn's bedroom either, but she could not stop thinking of how she had felt when he had looked into her eyes.

There were so many reasons that she should reject

the thoughts she was having. First and foremost, he was a loyal employee of her brother and did not have her best interests at heart.

Of course, Peg's husband had been an employee as well, or had at least pretended to be so. If the scraps of information she'd gleaned from Hugh were true, it appeared that they had survived their class differences and were managing happily together.

The most important reason to put thoughts of Michael Solomon aside was that he had done nothing to make her think that her feelings were reciprocated. He had insisted that he did not believe in love and seemed to have no interest in marrying. He had admitted to being fond of her, but one kiss and a few smouldering glances were no sign that an offer was pending. They were not even a guarantee of a second kiss.

If she wanted such a kiss, she would have to make an effort to put herself in the way of it, and that meant spending more time with the man who was fascinating her. He was probably in the garden right now, waiting for her to try and escape the house.

Of course, there was no rule that said she should not enjoy the garden as well. She went to the kitchen to gather scraps, then went outside under the guise of giving the dogs their breakfast. As she'd expected, Mr Solomon was there, on his usual bench beneath the tree, reading a book.

When she was done feeding the dogs, she sauntered

down the garden path. But, instead of standing before him, she took a seat beside him on the bench.

He looked up, surprised, but said nothing.

'Is it so unusual that I wish to enjoy the garden as much as you do?' she asked.

'Not really,' he replied. 'It has not happened before, of course, but, as you say, it is your garden and you can do what you like in it.' Then he went back to his book.

For a few moments she admired the flowers in front of them, contemplating her next move. Then she stole a glance in his direction and asked, 'What are you reading today?'

'A history of Persia.' He set it aside with a sigh and stared at her. 'Is there something I can help you with?'

'Every time I see you, you are reading,' she said.

'Not always,' he said, dismissing her attempt at conversation.

'Often enough,' she insisted, refusing to be shaken off. 'Are the books always histories?'

'Not always,' he admitted. 'But I am interested in learning about places that I am not likely to see.'

She stared straight ahead again. 'I can understand that. There are so many places that I will never visit.'

'Gretna Green, for one,' he said with a grin.

At one time it would have made her angry, but today she smiled back at him. 'I mean places much closer than that. When was the last time you danced, Mr Solomon?'

He thought for a moment. 'About a month ago. I attended a subscription dance at a small assembly room.

Nothing so prodigious as Almack's, of course. But suitable to pass an evening in genteel entertainment.'

She sighed. 'For me, it has been two years, six months and twenty-seven days.'

He started in surprise.

She stared down at the toes of her slippers. 'I recorded it in my diary. I wish I had written more detail, for I can barely remember it now.'

'Did Clement never take you dancing in all this time sneaking about?'

'We have managed stolen hours together,' she said with another sigh. 'But nothing so prolonged as to allow dancing.' Then she smiled, remembering. 'Of course, we had a dancing master for a time. But he turned out to be nothing more than a sham who wished to search our house. And then he married my sister.'

'Castell?' he said, surprised.

Olivia nodded. 'There was really no opportunity to dance with him either.'

'Perhaps, if you ask him, your brother will take you to Almack's, or some such,' he said, looking apprehensive.

She shook her head. 'After all this time, you still misunderstand how things are for me. If I went to Almack's, even while supervised by Hugh, I might meet a man who would wish to marry me. Hugh does not want me to marry. Therefore, there will be no Almack's for me.'

'And I suppose you have never tried to sneak out without his permission,' he said with a wry smile.

'Even I would not risk an indiscretion so great. It is one thing to run away with Alister. At least then I would have an escort, should I need help. But I would need vouchers for Almack's and Hugh has refused them. Even if I was able to procure one, it would surely get back to my brother that I had gone there, and he would see to it that I never left the house again.'

'Perhaps if you wore a disguise,' he suggested.

She shook her head. 'The dress code at Almack's is very strict. Evening gowns and gloves. Anything other than that and they would turn me away at the door. And I know of no one who is planning to hold a fancy dress ball this season. Even if they were, my brother would dispose of the invitation before I ever saw it.'

'You would not be out of place in a domino and mask at Vauxhall Gardens,' he said, then fell silent as if he realised that he should not be making such suggestions.

'I have never been there,' she said wistfully. 'But I have heard it is a most wondrous place. They have jugglers and balloon launches…'

'And dancing,' he added.

It also had unlit walkways where lovers met in darkness. Maybe he had forgotten that it was the last place he should be suggesting to a cloistered young lady. Or maybe he knew exactly what he was suggesting. 'Could you take me?' she said, reaching out a hand to tug gently on his sleeve. 'On some night when my brother is dining at his club, and you are supposed to be watching me.'

'I am supposed to be preventing such escapades,' he reminded her. 'It is the whole point of my job.'

'You are supposed to be preventing me from eloping, and I have no intention of doing that. If I stayed with you the whole time, you would be sure that nothing happened to me,' she said. 'It is not as if I would be meeting a stranger there. I will know no one but you.'

'Only me,' he said in a dazed voice.

'It would not be that much different than taking me to Bond Street,' she said.

'I suppose a short visit would do you no harm,' he agreed. 'If you will promise not to run away for at least a week after. I must gain some advantage for the risk I am taking, after all.'

'I would be no trouble at all to you for at least a week,' she said, giving him her most brilliant smile.

'All right then,' he said. 'Your brother will have my hide if he learns of this.'

'Then we must make sure that he does not,' she said, smiling. 'I will have my maid find a mask and hood for me to wear. Then I will come down to the garden to meet you. I shall have my adventure and we will be back in the house before anyone misses me.'

'Do not make me regret this,' he said, giving her a stern look.

'I will not,' she whispered and, because it seemed like the most natural thing in the world, she leaned in to kiss him on the cheek. Then she ran for the house before she could see his reaction to it.

* * *

A maid appeared in the doorway as she reached the house and Lady Olivia gestured over her shoulder at something in the garden, then turned and stared past him with an expression that said his presence in her life was too unimportant to acknowledge.

It probably was. He should not take what had just happened as truth and this sudden rejection as the lie. She had been all smiles and batted lashes when she had thought to get something from him, and he had fallen for it like a schoolboy whose stones had just dropped. And then she had rewarded him with a kiss.

She had pecked his cheek as if they were old friends and such intimacy was a common thing between them. But the simple act had undone him like Cupid's arrow. He wanted to take her to Vauxhall, or anywhere else she wanted to go. But not as some damned watchdog. He wanted to escort her, like the gentleman who should be taking her there.

Of course, she would likely use this outing as an excuse to meet Clement, and he would be played for the fool he was.

In any case, it was too late to rescind the offer, even if he wanted to. The prospect of an evening under the stars with the light of a hundred lanterns flickering in her blonde hair made his mouth water and his body tighten. He would give her the dance she was requesting, leading her through the figures and perhaps daring a waltz. It would be magic. He could be a man and not a lackey for an hour or two, with the most beautiful girl in England on his arm.

And then he would bring her home, and the spell would be broken. But, before that happened, he might earn another kiss better than the one he had just had. There was candlelight and moonlight at Vauxhall, but there was darkness as well, deep enough to conceal a multitude of sins.

'Where are you going, my lady?' Two days later, Molly was fluttering nervously around her as Liv gazed in the cheval glass and admired the hooded cape and mask she wore in preparation for going out.

'You are better off not knowing,' she said, giving her maid a narrow-eyed look.

'The Duke will not be happy if he hears of it,' the girl insisted.

'Then he had best not hear of it,' she said, staring daggers at Molly until she blanched. 'I do not want you tattling to my brother, or the other servants. If you do, I will see to it that more harm comes to you than will ever come to me.'

'Yes, my lady,' the girl said nervously.

'And you have nothing to worry about,' Liv assured her, sweetening her tone. 'It is not as if I am running away again. I will be back before midnight and will be properly escorted the whole time. No harm will have come from this.'

'If you are sure, my lady. Because I could lose my position...'

Liv sighed. 'I will see that you do not.' Because she would not be caught. The cape obscured her hair and body so completely that she doubted even her own sister would recognise her, should they meet. With a final glance in the mirror, she turned and left the room, hurrying down the main stairs and along the back hall towards the door to the garden.

Once outside, she saw Mr Solomon, nothing more than a tall shadow standing guard at the back gate. She opened her mouth to greet him and, as if he could see her intention in the darkness, he held up a hand, warning her to silence, opening the gate and shepherding her through.

Once on the street, he walked her to a waiting carriage, handed her up into the lit body and climbed in after her, signalling the driver to set off.

She pulled back her hood and lowered her mask, turning to stare out through the window at the darkened streets passing by outside. Then she turned back to him, bouncing in her seat. 'We are really going.'

'I said we would,' he agreed with a smile and a shrug.

'It is just... It has been so long,' she said, a lump rising in her throat.

'It is barely a week since your last trip towards Scotland,' he reminded her.

'But that was in broad daylight,' she reminded him. 'Night-time is very different.'

'If you say so,' he replied. She could see him shaking his head in the shadow of the corner.

'And on that trip I did nothing but ride and wait,' she said. 'The same as on the trip before that. Nothing else happened, either time.'

'Really?' he said in a voice full of doubt.

'What are you implying?' she said, honestly not sure.

Perhaps it was just the shadows falling across his face, but his expression was unreadable. 'Do you mean to tell me that Clement did not attempt to take liberties on either of your trips out of London?'

'Of course not,' she said, straightening her skirts. 'He is a gentleman.'

'He is a fool,' Mr Solomon responded. 'To miss such an opportunity, that is.'

'We have never…' She stopped, unsure what to say. She did not want to sound so prim that he would think she'd object to a few kisses, if they were taken by the right gentleman. But neither should she be encouraging anything to happen. She must accept that this trip was no more than something offered by one friend to another.

Surprisingly, she had no trouble thinking of Mr Solomon as a friend. Unlike the other men set to watch her, he had been kind and understanding, even when he had stood between her and what she had thought that she wanted more than anything in the world.

The real question was, would he ever want to be more than a friend?

She sighed, and said at last, 'My relationship with Alister has not progressed to the point you seem to think it has. And, looking back on his behaviour at the inn, I think it may be for the best.'

'I see.'

Did she detect pleasure in that short sentence? Perhaps it was just satisfaction that he had performed his job successfully. But she wanted it to be more than that.

'I heard Hugh tell his valet not to expect him back until tomorrow,' she said, changing the subject. Then she baited the hook. 'We can stay out as late as we wish.'

'No later than midnight,' he said, ignoring her offer. 'There is nothing but trouble to be had by staying out until dawn, and I am here as your protector, not your accomplice.'

'Midnight,' she agreed, checking her little gold watch. 'It is just eight now. Much can happen in four hours.'

'I certainly hope not,' he said, still smiling.

A short while later the carriage pulled up before the entrance to the Vauxhall pleasure garden. Mr Solomon jumped out before her, handing her down to the ground and escorting her past the ticket booth and onto the grounds.

'It is a marvel,' she said, staring at a lady in a spangled dress doing tricks on the back of a trained horse.

When she looked up, he was staring down at her, his gaze focused on her lips. 'Indeed.' Then he looked away quickly, as if to prove he was as fascinated by the performance as she had been.

She grabbed his sleeve, tugging him further into the venue towards the place she most wanted to see. 'Show me everything,' she said, turning around and trying to take it all in.

'Then let us begin at the music pavilion,' he said. 'You wanted to dance, did you not?'

'Please,' she said, tipping her head to catch the distant sound of a waltz.

He walked her towards it, leading her all the way out onto the dance floor, where he held out his hands to her.

'You want to dance with me?' she said hopefully.

'You did not think I would allow you to dance with strangers, did you?' he said, making it all sound quite sensible. 'What kind of a chaperone would I be if I let you out of my keeping in that way? You might have arranged for Clement to spirit you away and I could do little to stop it.'

'I did not,' she said, incensed.

'All the same, if you wish to dance, it had best be with me,' he replied.

He made it sound like a reasonable plan, something done to keep her safe. She would accept that if it was all that he would offer. But it would have been so much nicer had he really wanted to dance with her, rather than telling her it was his duty.

And now that she was in his arms on the dance floor, all reservations were forgotten. When she had been out, two years ago, she'd not had permission to waltz. To have her first one be with a man she dreamed of made it all the more precious.

There was something faintly intimidating about Mr Solomon, which probably explained the shiver travelling up and down her spine. Standing close to him, he was taller than she remembered, and she could not help noticing how broad his shoulders were. He was graceful, and his lead was masterful in a way she had never experienced before. She could follow a man like this anywhere he might take her. She leaned her head back to look up at him, then back further as they spun, to watch the first fireworks going off above the lantern-lit trees.

'Another dance?' he asked as the song ended and the next one began.

'Oh, please,' she said, and they joined a circle for a country dance. That was followed by a gavotte, and then another waltz. They were both exhausted by the time he led her down a path to see the jugglers. And from there it was refreshments in the Turkish saloon and a walk through the triumphal arches, and over a small bridge where they threw the last of their sandwiches to the ornamental carp in the little pond.

She looked ahead to the place where the lanterns seemed to stop, leaving the path in shadow. 'Is that the place I have heard of?' she asked. 'Where lovers go to meet?'

'The dark walks,' he said, pulling her up short to turn her away.

'I want to see,' she said, pulling away again.

'And you cannot,' he replied. 'If only because it is dark, and you can see nothing in that.'

'Next, you will tell me that it is improper,' she replied, scoffing.

'Because it is,' he agreed, gently taking hold of her arm. 'There is a reason that chaperones do not allow their charges down those paths.'

'Well, I have nothing to worry about,' she said. 'There is no one I intend to meet there, and you are here to keep me from getting into trouble.' Then she broke free of his grasp and ran down the path into the darkness.

She heard him sigh and set off after her, a few paces behind.

For a place as shocking as this was supposed to be, it was disappointing that Mr Solomon had been right about there being nothing much to see. But that was the thing about darkness. It obscured. Even after her eyes began to adjust to the gloom, she wasn't able to make out more than a few isolated shapes. There were trees and hedges on either side of the path which she felt beneath her feet. And there were occasional darker patches that were most likely small clearings with benches or follies where one might stop to…

She was not sure exactly what. It was probably nothing beyond a few stolen kisses, since she found it hard to believe that even the bravest couples would attempt anything more in such a public place.

But when she strayed too near one of them, she heard a female gasp and a sharp male curse, followed by the rustle of clothing and a warning to move on.

She jumped as she felt Mr Solomon come up behind and take her arm, pulling her away from the couple she had interrupted and deeper into the darkness.

'Are you satisfied?' he asked. 'It is nothing but more of the same, from here to the end of the walk.'

They were beside another bench, and this one was unoccupied. She was sure because she could make out the uninterrupted white of the marble in the gloom. 'Let us stop and sit for a while before going back,' she said, plopping herself down on the seat and dragging him down with her.

'If you want to rest, there are plenty of places in the lighted portion of the park,' he said. 'This place is for other activities.' There was something more than resignation in his voice, something lush and promising that sent another shiver through her body.

'I wanted an adventure,' she said, smiling to herself. 'Even if nothing more happens tonight, this is more adventurous than I had ever expected to be.'

In the silence after her words she could hear a new sort of night sound around them, other than the whisper of the wind in the leaves and the calls of night birds. She could hear murmured words of love, sighs, giggles and the sounds of bodies moving against bodies.

She was conscious of the feel of Mr Solomon's shoulder leaning into hers as they sat together. The bench was small, as if designed to force intimacy on those who shared it. It made her feel curiously vulnerable and yet strangely brave. Without thinking, she reached out for her companion's hand.

When she touched him, he did not pull away. But he did say, 'This is extremely unwise, Lady Olivia.'

'You may call me Liv,' she said. 'The situation does not call for such formality.' She hesitated for a moment and then asked, 'What shall I call you?'

'Michael. Until we return to the light, at least. Then it would be wiser to forget I even have a Christian name.'

'As you wish, Michael,' she said and felt him shiver at her side. 'Tell me, have you come here with other women?'

'When I was young and foolish I attempted it, once or twice,' he said. 'Fortunately, the girls said no. If they'd agreed, I'd likely be married by now.'

'Do all men marry the girls they take here?' she said, surprised.

'If they are caught, they would have no choice,' he replied. 'If they wanted to be thought of as gentlemen.'

'And is that how you wish to be thought of?' she asked.

'I know my place, Liv,' he said. 'But I also know better than to be indiscreet.'

'Oh,' she said softly, unsure why it disappointed her to know that he was an honest man.

'Are you not concerned with your reputation?' he said.

'No one will know I was here,' she reminded him,

before pulling off her mask and brushing it against the back of his hand. 'Even undisguised, I doubt my old friends would recognise me if they saw me. Most of them are married now, and not having liaisons in a pleasure garden.' She thought for a moment. 'Since my first season was three years ago, I am practically on the shelf.'

At this, he laughed. 'You make it sound as if you are too old to interest a man.'

'To interest the men who once courted me,' she said, quite sure of herself. 'Many of those married my friends. The rest are at Almack's tonight, courting girls fresh out of the schoolroom.'

'Except for Clement,' he reminded her.

'I did not think you liked him,' she reminded him.

'I do not,' he agreed. 'You deserve better.' He turned towards her now, leaning closer. 'If he were any kind of man, you'd have been married over a year ago. Despite what you claim, he has probably taken enough liberties with your virtue that he feels no urgent need to make it right between you.'

'That is a terrible thing to say,' she said. 'I have… We have… I mean, a few kisses, of course. But…' He had done nothing like the things she suspected were happening all around her, even as they spoke.

'Let us see, shall we?' He leaned the rest of the way in, and suddenly his lips were on hers and his hands circled her waist.

She gasped in shock, for his kiss was nothing like

the ones she had had before. When Alister kissed her it sometimes felt that he had no interest in what she might feel in response. But Michael Solomon's kiss seemed calculated to raise an answer from her. He was toying with her lips, tracing them with his tongue as his fingers closed possessively on her waist, pulling her closer to him.

She should resist. She should demand that he stop. But wasn't this what she had been hoping for when she'd set off into the darkness? She'd wanted to find somewhere where society's rules did not apply. As far as she could tell, this was the only such place she would ever be allowed to enter.

So she sighed, put her hands on his shoulders to steady herself against him and gave in to the pleasure. It was very nice indeed. His lips were firm and warm and he tasted of the spiced nuts they'd bought from a vendor in the Turkish Pavilion.

And, most shocking of all, he had slipped his tongue between her barely parted lips and was moving it around inside her mouth. At first, she had no idea what she was to do. Alister had done the same to her on several occasions but had expected nothing in return. In fact, he seemed to prefer that she remain passive.

But Michael seemed to want more. He would move for a bit and then stop, as if he had asked a question and was expecting an answer. And all the while the hands that had moved to her back were stroking, as if in encouragement.

Gingerly, she moved her tongue as he had done, then thrust hesitantly into his mouth and did the same. She could feel the lips touching hers smile in approval as he began to move with more purpose.

The kiss raised strange feelings in her, a fluttering uncertainty that she rarely felt when she was with Alister. She stretched her arms outward and wrapped them around his neck, swaying against him and opening her mouth wider, offering anything he wished to take.

He pulled away briefly, his tongue tracing the shell of her ear. 'Perhaps you are telling me the truth. You certainly do not seem like you have been kissed properly before.' Then his hand strayed from her back to her side, to her bosom.

This was different from the furtive touches she had experienced so far in her life. This was a commanding caress, pressing hard enough against her body to find the nipples protected by her stays. He moved his hand just enough to arouse them to hard beads of pleasure, making her moan in excitement.

He laughed softly before kissing her again and releasing her. 'All right, I believe you. Your lover is faint of heart and affection if he has not given you this small amount of pleasure.'

She pulled away. 'Was that all this was? A test of my virtue?'

'Or lack of it,' he teased. Then added in a more serious tone, 'Perhaps that was how it began. But that is not how it will end.' Then he kissed her again, and his previous effort paled in comparison. His mouth seemed to envelop hers, stealing her soul with each breath they took together. His hands roamed freely over her body, memorising each curve until she felt hot and ready to strip the gown from her body, to lie naked in the moonlight and let him do what he would with her.

She wanted to feel him as well, trailing her hands down his chest, pushing her fingers inside his waistcoat and letting one hand drop into his lap to cup the hard bulge of his erection.

She immediately regretted it for he jumped away from her in surprise, taking in deep gulps of air as if he had been underwater and was just returning to the surface. Then he stood up, taking a step away from the bench. 'I think that is enough of an experiment for the evening, Lady Olivia.'

'Experiment?' she said, annoyed at the faint tremor of embarrassment in her voice.

'You wanted to experience the dark walks,' he said. 'Now you have. It is probably close to midnight, and time to return home before you are missed.'

'Hugh said he would be gone all night,' she reminded him. 'No one will ever know.'

'I will know,' he said, and there was no trace of the softness that had been in his voice as he'd kissed her. 'And I say it is time to go.'

They had been having a lovely time. Then it had been even better. And then she had ruined everything.

'Of course,' she said, pulling her cloak tight around her body and feeling vulnerable and foolish.

He was walking away without her and she stood and hurried down the path to catch him up. 'You will not tell anyone what we have done?' she said.

'God, no. Do you take me for a fool?' He sounded disgusted. But whether with her or himself, she was not sure.

They had reached the edge of the darkness and were continuing down the path towards the exit when she heard a voice in front of her snarl, 'What the devil? Olivia? You are not allowed to be out of the house.'

It was Hugh. How had he recognised her? She reached up to touch her face and realised she'd forgotten the mask she had removed during the last minutes in the darkness.

'She should not have got this far,' Michael said in a voice that was disapproving but revealed no trace of the reality that had passed between them. 'I am to blame for that. But there was no sign of whomever she intended to meet.'

It was a necessary lie. But it hurt that he could so easily deny her. She could not stop her response. 'I was not meeting anyone. I came here for my own pleasure.'

'If I were to believe that it would be even worse,' Hugh snapped, glaring at her. 'That would mean that you have been wandering about London at night with no chaperone at all. We will discuss what you have or have not done tomorrow, when we are both home.'

'And just what are you doing here?' she said, sensing an opening in the argument that could be exploited. It was then she noticed that a woman was standing just behind him, as shrouded in disguise as Liv had been and doing her best to pretend that she was not a part of the argument in progress. 'Who is your friend?' Liv asked, craning to see around him and offering an insincere smile to his companion. 'I do not believe you mentioned where you were going when you left tonight, or where you might be. You only said that you did not mean to come home.'

The woman he was with stiffened and gasped and it was clear that, whatever Hugh's plans might have been, hers did not include a liaison that lasted past sunrise. She turned, running up the path behind them.

Hugh reached for her, his mouth forming the beginning of a name and then stopping as he realised that the point of secrecy was not to call out to a person so all within earshot would learn their identity. He turned back to Liv for only a moment, glaring at her before snapping at Michael to, 'Take her home immediately and see that she does not stray again.' Then he was off up the path after his escaping friend.

Once he was gone there was a moment's silence between them before Liv said, 'Well. That was interesting.'

'Interesting?' he said in much the same tone Hugh had used. 'We were very nearly caught by your brother, who, as you keep reminding me, has a penchant for homicide.'

'And you covered for us masterfully,' she said, not as embarrassed as she should have been by what had occurred between them. 'He'd never have guessed that it was you I was with all along.'

'Of course he wouldn't,' Michael said with a snarl. 'Because I am so far beneath you that you could not possibly have allowed me to do what I did.'

'That is not what I meant,' she insisted, realising that she'd hurt him.

'On the contrary, I understand you better than you do yourself,' he said. 'Things are quite different in the dark than they are in the light, aren't they?'

'Did you want me to acknowledge you?' she asked, just as angry as he was. 'That would have meant an end to your position, at the minimum. We'd have never seen each other again.'

'That would have been the best for both of us,' he replied. 'If your protector was sacked, it would leave you free to run off with Clement. And it has given you leverage to use against me with your brother. If I do something you do not like, you have but to tell him that I was pawing at you in the shadows of Vauxhall.'

The idea had never occurred to her. It made what they had done together seem cheap and dishonourable. 'Clearly, your mind runs in the gutter and cannot think anything but the worst of me,' she said. 'Before, you thought me unchaste. Now, you think me a blackmailer.

To be clear, if I wanted to level accusations against you, I would not need to have kissed you. I could simply have accused you of things you had not done, and my brother would take my side against you.'

He grabbed her by the wrist, pulling her towards the gate. 'Then I am glad that I have at least got some pleasure from you before you began telling tales. My only regret is that I did not give you what you were panting for back there. If I am going to hang in the morning, I might as well be guilty of the crime.'

He was hauling her towards the waiting carriage. When they arrived at it, he shoved her inside and hesitated on the step for a moment before giving the driver curt instructions and climbing in after her.

Now that they were alone together, the silence in the coach was oppressive. When she could not stand it any longer, she announced, 'Since you find me so detestable, you do not have to come with me. I am quite capable of getting down and through my own gate without your help.'

'Even now, you do not understand,' he said. 'It is my job to see that you are home and safe. I am doing that job to the best of my ability. And what happened at Vauxhall…' He gave a disgusted wave of his hand. 'I am not some plaything to be used and discarded when you are no longer amused.'

'I never thought you were, Michael,' she said quietly.

He flinched at the sound of his own name and replied, 'What occurred tonight will not happen again.

I think, in the future, our relationship should return to that which you had with previous guards that your brother hired. I will stay on one side of the door, and you on the other.'

He settled back in his seat and looked out of the window then, offering not another word for the rest of the trip.

## Chapter Eleven

Michael wished he could have thought of the night's activities as a good plan gone bad. But, from the first, he had known it was a disaster in the making. He should not have been dancing with her. He should not have gone anywhere near the dark walks. And he should not have done anything that might have been discovered by the Duke of Scofield.

Worst of all, he should not have enjoyed it. Lord, but she had been sweet in the darkness, where he could pretend that she was just a woman and he was just a man. But seeing her brother had brought reality crashing back. There was no way that she would forget his lowly position on her brother's staff long enough to want anything more than a flirtation. Nor could he continue to dally with an innocent, no matter how responsive she was to his advances.

His only hope was that, on his arrival the following morning, the Duke would fire him out of hand. Then he would not have to see her again, nor would he have to stand by as she either succeeded in marrying the unworthy Clement, or whatever man her brother would eventually choose for her.

To think the matter over, he went to the nearest pub he could find. Since it required a lot of thinking, he tried a gin mill as well. And since it was hard to think in the din there, he found a gambling hell where he could lose the remainder of the money in his purse.

Then he walked towards his home, trying not to think at all about the woman he had left behind, and the chance that she might have escaped in the night, despite what she had told him. Tomorrow—or was it today?—he would be in no condition to outpace her should she make a run for the Scottish border.

He was not aware of the sound of running feet behind him until the stranger was almost upon him. He turned at the last second and the knife that had been inches from his back grazed his arm instead, slicing easily through the wool of his coat and splitting the sleeve and skin beneath.

He batted the arm that held it with his other hand, then lunged forward with the full weight of his body, knocking his assailant off-balance and into the street. Before he could get a good look at his attacker, a horse and cart passed between them.

When it was gone, so was the thief. For that was who it must have been: a cutpurse waiting outside the gambling hell to take advantage of drunken winners. The poor fellow had chosen unwisely. Though Michael would not deny being in his cups, he had been losing steadily for hours.

\* \* \*

By the time he returned to Gracechurch Street he was bruised and bloody and it was nearly nine in the morning. But at least he had forgotten what it was that worried him.

It had something to do with work, he was sure. He was in no condition to go there, so dealing with it would have to wait until he'd had a wash and a few hours' sleep.

But when he entered the house, instead of peace and quiet, he was greeted with a foyer full of chests and trunks, and the housekeeper and footman bustling about the room, clearly in a tizzy. His mother waded into the midst of it, tapping the tops of the baggage and indicating the order that they should be carried to the wagon that was waiting at the front door. Even more strange than the activity taking place was his mother's attire. In place of the severe black gowns he was accustomed to, she wore a fashionable day dress of brilliant blue silk, the white organza chemisette closed at the throat with a delicate brooch of opal and pearls.

'What the devil is going on?' Michael said, standing in the way, only to be nudged to the side by two grunting servants carrying a large box.

'I wanted to tell you,' his mother said, tossing her hands in the air to signify her frustration. 'But you have been so busy lately. And I did not think you would understand.'

'You are right,' he said. 'I do not understand. Where do you think you are going?'

John Solomon appeared from the sitting room, standing at her side. 'She is going to my house, where she belongs.'

'John's place is much larger, you see,' she said, blushing slightly. 'Not that you have not offered me more than I'd ever hoped for in the way of a home. But your father is eager to share his good fortune with me, and to make up for the time we were apart.'

'My father?' If he'd even believed the man existed, much less lived, it still would have been strange to see his mother disappear with the man after just a few days. 'You are moving to his residence?'

'It is time that you had your own home without the trouble of housing me,' she added with a concerned look, then leaned forward to surreptitiously sniff his breath. She made no comment on the ruined coat or the trickle of blood running down the back of his hand, other than to give him a disappointed shake of her head.

'It is no trouble to keep you here,' he said irritably. 'It never was.'

'Of course not,' Solomon replied. 'And you have cared well for your mother in my absence. But now that I am back, I am eager to take on the duty.'

'And it will be easier, for all of us, if your father and I keep our own house and you keep yours.' There passed a look between the two older people in the room that was unmistakably intimate. Then his mother gave him an encouraging look. 'I am sure, sooner if not later, there will be a woman in this house that will take my place. I have been interfering in your life far too long. It is past time that you marry and start your own family.'

'I do not want or need a wife and children,' he said, annoyed at the slurring in his voice. Drunk or sober, he did not now, nor had he ever believed in love. Even so, he could not help imagining Liv walking down the stairs on his left, greeting him upon his homecoming.

'It has been a very long time that we have been apart,' Solomon said, beaming at his wife. 'We have much to…talk about.'

His mother giggled.

His father continued. 'We will stay a few months in my house on Grosvenor Square…'

'Not far from Scofield and his sister,' his mother added.

'How delightful,' Michael said, feeling the beginnings of a headache.

His father ignored the interruptions and continued. 'Until we can find a place that suits us both to build a manor in the country. And then, if Maria wishes it, we shall travel.' He stared at her fondly. 'Now that I have found her, she shall see all the wonders I have seen, and have every happiness I can give her.'

'I see,' Michael said, as his temples began to throb. 'But you have been apart for thirty years.' He stared at John Solomon. 'Before that, you were together for a year or less. Why do you think to set up house after all this time?'

'Because we love each other,' Solomon said.

'Surely you must have known that,' his mother said in a tone that was almost a scold. 'I have told you often enough about our time together. And never for a moment of the time we were apart did my love for John dim one iota from what it was.'

'Yes, but…' Michael began and then stopped. She had said all those things, of course. And he had not believed one of them. He had assumed that his mother's feelings were some sort of delusion created to camouflage her dishonour, and to give him hope that his absent father had not disappeared as soon as he'd realised that she was with child.

The fact that all she'd told him had been true was a situation he had never imagined.

'There will be space for you to visit, if you wish it,' his father said, still not taking his eyes off the woman he had been searching for, as if afraid that she might disappear if he looked away. 'After you have given us a chance to get settled.'

By the look on his face, getting settled was a euphemism for something that Michael did not want to think about regarding his own mother. 'That is all right. This house is quite suitable for my needs,' he said, rubbing his temples.

'I knew you would understand,' his mother said, looking at him briefly before turning to the man at her side. 'It is all very sudden, of course. But we have been apart for so long and I've missed John terribly. We want to make up for all those lost years in any way we can.'

'Just go,' he said, cutting off what was likely to be a repetition of their everlasting love. 'I do not need to visit. I do not need either of you. Just go.' Then he stalked into the study, to search for the brandy bottle.

That morning Liv's brother was waiting for her at the table in the breakfast room, a slice of toast in his hand and a stern expression on his face.

She ignored it and seated herself, pouring chocolate and slathering jam on a slice of bread as if it were the only thing in the world that mattered to her.

'Are you going to explain yourself?' he said when the silence between them had gone on long past comfort.

'What are you referring to?' she said, trying to ignore the knife in his hand as he buttered his toast.

'What were you doing in Vauxhall Gardens? Who did you intend to meet? And how did you evade Solomon yet again?' He gestured broadly with the knife. 'I hired the fellow to keep ahead of you, not lag one step behind. He is worse than useless if he cannot keep you in the house as I requested.'

He was also not at his usual post in the garden when she had looked for him. But it was best not to call attention to that fact when her brother was in a mood to sack someone. 'Michael is doing his job quite well, I should think. I am still here, aren't I?'

'Michael, is it?' her brother said, as if one word encompassed the whole of the problem.

'Mr Solomon,' she corrected too late.

'Let us be clear on the matter. Michael Solomon is in my employ to prevent you from leaving the house, not to bring you back when you have already run away. I did not hire him to fetch and carry for you on Bond Street. Nor did I expect you to become overly familiar with him.'

'I am not overly familiar with him,' she said, trying not to think of what they had done, alone in the darkness. 'But you have me trapped in this house and he is the only one of any education to whom I can speak. Do you mean to deny me all intellectual stimulation?'

'It is not your intellect I am worrying about,' he said with a sarcastic smile.

'I don't understand what you mean,' she said, giving him her best blank look.

'Then let me put it to you clearly. After two years of droning on about the fellow, you have not mentioned Alister Clement in days. And yet you are calling your guard by his Christian name. You are forming an attachment to him, and I will not have it.'

'Really, Hugh,' she said, forcing a laugh. 'I knew you were jealous of my fondness for Alister. But now you are fixing your mind on any man I speak to and imagining nonsense.'

His hand tightened on the knife he held until his knuckles went white. 'You are trying to twist my concern against me, but you have only proved my point. You have never before spoken to the men I hired to guard you. Not until Solomon arrived. You should not have been near him at all. I do not want you seeking opportunities to turn him to your will and convince him that his job is to obey you and not the man who hired him.'

She blinked. 'Then why are you barking at me and not him? If what he has done is so horrible…' She paused, shutting her mouth before finishing the sentence. She had almost suggested that Michael Solomon be fired. After what had happened, she could not bear the thought that she might lose him. She moderated her tone. 'Well, I promise that I have not been doing anything like what you seem to be imagining,' she said at last, trying to turn the conversation. 'And while we are discussing last night, who was the woman you were with?'

'What woman?' he said, too quickly to be sincere.

'The one who was masked, and who ran away once she realised who you were talking to,' Liv said, enjoying her brother's obvious embarrassment.

'That is none of your business,' Hugh said when he could not seem to come up with either a truth or a convincing lie.

'Were you going to spend the night with her?' Liv asked, honestly interested. Before Peg had disappeared, she had been convinced that her brother had lost his heart to someone. 'Was she your mistress?'

'You should not even know of such things, much less ask about them,' Hugh replied.

'She could not have been a mistress,' Liv said

thoughtfully. 'A Cyprian would not have bothered with a disguise.' That meant that she was someone's wife, or a lady who did not want to be seen unchaperoned with Liv's notorious brother.

'Stop speculating,' he said, getting up from the table and throwing his napkin down. 'The woman does not concern you. Nor will either of us be seeing her again.' There was something in his face as he said it that had nothing to do with his previous anger at her. Whoever it was, he had lost her when she had run from him. Before Liv had interrupted them, they had been heading for the dark walk that she had just come from. And she was not sure how, but somehow she had spoiled everything.

'I am sorry,' she said, watching him carefully, trying to understand. 'I am not sure what I have done exactly, and I know that you will never tell me. But I ruined your evening by appearing when I did.'

He dropped back into his seat with a sigh. 'Do not blame yourself for it. It was a mistake from the start.'

'Is she the reason you have never married?' she asked. 'Peg was under the impression that you had found and lost your true love.'

'Peg was too nosy for her own good,' he said.

She gasped. 'You did not do anything to her, did you? Please say you did not punish her for leaving.'

He stared at her in shock. 'Do you really think so little of me?' He shook his head. 'To the best of my knowledge, your sister is fine. And as for the woman you saw with me last night? I should have known better than to meet her. What we have… What we *had* is not something that can be regained. In the future, let us both pretend that yesterday evening did not happen.'

She doubted that she would forget, for even with the interruption it had been the best night of her life. But it would be easier for all of them if she could pretend that it did not matter to her. 'Very well,' she said, staring down into her tea and dreaming of Vauxhall.

## Chapter Twelve

It was after noon before Michael took his usual place under the tree in the Scofield garden. He had enquired after the Duke and was relieved to hear that the peer was already gone from the house. He had expected a dressing-down for the incident at Vauxhall, or at least a reprimand for arriving late. Apparently, he'd got a reprieve.

But the Duke was, by far, the lesser of his two problems. What was he going to do about Liv? The fact that he had kissed her was, at a minimum, a breach of duty. It was worse that he had taken advantage of a girl who was clearly an innocent, and even worse that he wanted to do it again, despite all the arguments he could make against that.

It didn't matter what he wanted. This could not continue. He had no intention of offering her marriage, and would surely be refused if he did. Scofield would remind him that he was a lesser man than the one they both sought to protect her from. The idea that the Duke would sanction a marriage between them was ludicrous.

Instead, he would be sent from the house without another word.

And he did not want marriage, he reminded himself. He was born strong enough to be alone, had been so all his life, and would remain thus, content, until he died.

Of course now he had a family on Grosvenor Square...

He shook his head. He had said only this morning that he did not need help from his father or anyone else. Nor did he believe in the sort of tender emotions that made a man doubt his purpose and turn away from actual, attainable goals. Yet here he was, plotting a future with a woman he could not have.

It was madness.

He settled down under the tree, shielding his bloodshot eyes with his hat, and reached into his pocket for a book, hoping that the lady in question would stay inside and not bother him, at least until his mind had fully recuperated from their last time together.

In less than a quarter hour, however, he felt the shadow fall across his face and caught the gentle scent of her perfume.

'Where were you?' she asked, not bothering with greetings or apologies.

'This morning?' he said without opening his eyes. 'I took the liberty of sleeping in. It was a late night, after all, Lady Olivia.'

'You were to call me Liv,' she reminded him.

'In another time and another place,' he replied.

'Just over twelve hours ago,' she said. 'You make it sound like an eternity.'

It felt like one. 'A lot has happened since then,' he said.

'Not to me.' She sat down next to him, forcing her way onto the bench and bumping against his injured arm.

He groaned.

'What is wrong?' Her hand came up to his shoulder, patting her way down his bicep until she touched the wound and he flinched.

'I had a small run-in with a cutpurse on the way home last night,' he said. 'I would like to say he got the worst of it, but that would be a lie.'

'You were attacked?' she said, horrified.

'It is a danger when one is on the street late at night.' He removed his hat and looked at her, since it was obvious that she did not mean to leave him alone.

'But with a knife,' she said. 'And after seeing my brother.'

'I am sure there is no connection,' he said, not sure at all.

'When we were in Bond Street,' she reminded him, 'there was the horse that almost ran you down. And the next day Hugh was angry because someone had seen us there.'

'A coincidence,' he said, thinking of the vague feelings of being watched, and the strange woman in the street who had warned him away from Liv.

She reached out and clasped his hands. 'I am so sorry. I did not mean for you to get hurt.'

'You were not the one to hurt me,' he said. 'And we have no proof that the things that happened to me were related. I have had worse weeks, working for other people.'

'But you are not working for someone else,' she said, looking increasingly worried. 'You are working for the Duke of Scofield, who has a history of removing obstacles with a knife.'

'Even if he does, it does not explain the incident with the horse,' Michael said, doing his best not to be swayed by her panic.

'If he was riding when he saw you with me, he'd have used whatever was at hand. And if one is caught, it would be easy to claim the incident was an accident, just as you are doing now.'

There was an annoying amount of logic behind her worry. If her brother was as dangerous and impulsive as she thought, things might have gone very like that. 'Did it look like his horse that struck me? Did you get a look at the rider?'

'No,' she admitted. 'I was too busy worrying about you.'

'And I you,' he agreed. 'But none of this is anything we need to obsess over. I was not badly hurt either time.'

'But what of the next time?' she said.

He took a deep breath. 'There will not be a next time, Lady Olivia.'

'Of course there will,' she said with a shocked laugh. 'It is not as if he will forget that he is angry with you.'

'He will not bother me because I mean to give him no reason for anger. Since it appears that Clement has learned his lesson, my job here is almost at an end. Until I am sure that I am no longer needed, there will be no more sponge cake and sorbet, and certainly no more trips down the dark walks.'

'Because you are afraid of my brother,' she said. 'I did not think you a coward.'

'I am not afraid of him,' he replied. 'I am simply aware that my job is a temporary position. You must remind yourself of that as well. If you are spinning fantasies that our acquaintance will last beyond a few weeks, you do not understand the situation at all.'

By the hurt look in her eyes, that was exactly what she had been doing. He could hardly blame her for clinging to the next available rescuer when Clement had failed her. But, for the sake of her honour, neither of them could afford to exaggerate his place in her future.

'I was always going to leave,' he said, watching her flinch. 'What happened between us at Vauxhall was a temporary diversion. You must never forget that. You will find that it changes the way you think of me. It will be easier that way.'

He had expected there would be tears. If there were, she was too proud to shed them in front of him. Without another word or a look in his direction, she stood and walked back into the house, closing the door behind her rather than slamming it.

He was leaving.

Not today, or tomorrow. But it was clear that the time in Vauxhall, which had been a profound experience for her, had meant little or nothing to him. He was casting her off after a few kisses, pretending that he felt nothing for her. Perhaps she was as naïve as he thought she was. But she was sure there was something more between them than the diversion he deemed it.

She had known it since the kiss he'd claimed was to stop her hysterics. A man who did not care would have slapped her, or at least given her a good shaking and a whiff of hartshorn. He had kissed her because he'd wanted to, the same as he had done at Vauxhall. And now he wanted to pretend that it would be as easy to end it as it was to start.

Hugh was just the same, claiming he wanted to forget what had happened when, actually, he had attempted to take revenge as soon as Liv was safely out of the way. It made things doubly dangerous for Michael that she had revealed her feelings for him at breakfast by using his proper name.

Everyone seemed to think she could take it all back and return to the way things were before she had met Michael Solomon. Perhaps she should try. Then she would not feel like a fool when she looked at Michael, nor would Hugh have reason to kill him.

She walked slowly up to her room, trying to imagine a life without Michael in it. He had been with her only a few weeks. Surely he was not indispensable. She had survived before without him. Without chess and conversation. Without laughter at Gunter's. Without kisses in the dark.

She had been going blindly forward towards her imagined happy marriage to Alister, sure life would be better than it had been here. But the last time he had taken her away from the house he had frightened her nearly to panic and had not even noticed. And the closer they'd got to elopement, the more nightmares she'd had.

Hadn't Michael told her that her choice was unworthy? Perhaps if Hugh had said something more than no and allowed her to go about with Alister, she'd have given him up years ago.

Instead, she'd had to meet a true gentleman to learn the difference between a man who was wrong for her and one who was right. She smiled. She knew what she wanted; now she simply had to convince Michael.

When she arrived at her room there was a letter placed squarely on the pillow of her bed. She frowned, knowing it was probably a note from Alister, outlining his next attempt at taking her away. It had no direction on the outside, or any other indication of the sender. It was sealed with red wax stamped with a rose and not the *A* signet she had seen hanging from the fob of Alister's watch chain.

She cracked the seal and unfolded the paper to see the words.

*STAY AWAY FROM SOLOMON*

She stared at the single line, printed in a large childish scrawl, and felt the room begin to tilt under her. The ink was red as blood, spattered in gory spots at the bottom of the page where a signature should be. The pen had gouged the paper on the downstrokes, making a series of open wounds.

Her breath was coming quickly, leaving her dizzy, and she grabbed the bedpost, eyes closed, gulping air until the urge to faint had passed. It was only ink. She, of all people, knew the difference between drying blood and an attempt to frighten.

'Molly!' She shouted for her maid, relieved to make a noise in anger, rather than the smothered scream of her dreams.

'My lady?' The girl was there in a moment, eyes wide with fear at the sight of her mistress, still pale and clinging to the furniture.

'Where did this come from?' She shook the paper in the air.

'A lady on the street,' the maid whispered. 'She handed it to me and said it was to come to you and no one else.'

'A woman?' she said, surprised.

The girl nodded. 'Did I do wrong? I thought it might be from Mr Clement.'

She was not even supposed to know about Alister.

But Liv should have known it was impossible to keep a real secret from one's maid. 'You did nothing wrong,' she said, pleased that she was able to gain control and keep her voice steady. 'Describe the woman, please.'

'I do not know,' Molly said with a worried shake of her head. 'I met her on the way back from a visit to my sister at Enderland's manor. Yesterday was my half day.'

Liv nodded encouragingly.

'She was cloaked, even though the day was warm. I think her hair was dark, but I am not sure.'

'Not sure.' She made one frustrated circuit of the room, then tossed the paper into the fire, watching it catch on the banked ashes and wither to nothing. 'If you see her again, do not accept any more notes from her.'

'Very good, my lady.'

Liv waved the girl away with a swish of her hand and stared at the ashes, thinking. Though Michael had said nothing of it, it appeared she had a rival for his affections. He was not married, she was sure. Nor was he seriously engaged. He had been far too honourable in their dealings so far for her to believe that he would play another woman false.

But the letter had decided her course of action. If she let things go back to the way they had been before she had met him, she would be all alone. And he would be lost to some dark-haired beauty with a hot temper.

She would prove to Hugh and Michael how wrong they both were. Hugh had given up trying to control Peg once she was married. If Liv could tie the knot before her brother realised it, he might have to concede. And if she wanted that marriage to be with Michael Solomon, she would need to get him alone and thinking about something other than the performance of his duties.

She smiled.

Perhaps it would be better if she forced him to do his job. If she ran, he would chase. It was what he was paid to do. Once he caught her, there would be the long hours together as he tried to bring her home. In that time, she would make him see the wonderful future that was possible if he would see her as a woman and not a responsibility.

She had but to choose the place, the time and the reason. She had promised that she would not decamp for at least a week, but promises were made to be broken. She must give it enough thought to have a decent plan.

Six days later, Liv placed a packet under her pillow, scrawled a note to Michael and then donned her simplest gown and walked out through the front door of the house, towards Scotland and freedom.

## Chapter Thirteen

'What do you mean, she is gone?' Michael ran a clawed hand through his hair, baffled as to how things could have spun from his control without his noticing.

For nearly a week Liv had been as obedient as he could have hoped. She had greeted him politely when she had come into the garden to feed the dogs, but she had made no more attempts to engage him in conversation. Nor had she flirted with him or made any effort to contact Alister Clement.

If he was honest, it was a little insulting. He had told her to forget about what had happened in Vauxhall, but he had not thought she would do it so easily. He'd put his best effort into the kisses he'd given her, and her response had kept him awake at night in his empty house, imagining an impossible future with her in it.

It enraged him to think that, after what they had done together, she was still able to think of Clement. She had promised him a week of peace. Instead, she had used the distance he'd placed between them to plot with her lover in secret. And he had been working so hard at staying out of her way and maintaining control over his unruly emotions that he'd let her trick him.

'Damn the woman!' he exploded.

The maid jumped in terror.

'What time did you miss her?' he demanded, changing his tone to something less likely to frighten the girl to silence. 'No one is blaming you for this, mind. I just need all the information I can gather to find your mistress and bring her home.'

'I went to wake her this morning, and she was nowhere to be found,' Molly the maid said, near to tears. 'I came to the room at nine, as I always do. And put her to bed at midnight.'

'Very good,' Michael said in an encouraging tone. 'And does the Duke know she is gone?'

'He did not come home last night,' she said.

Michael breathed a silent sigh of relief. It would be better for all concerned if Liv was back in the house before the Duke turned up. 'And you saw no one, other than Lady Olivia? There was no sign of Clement?'

'None,' the girl said. 'But she left you a note.'

He held out a hand, snapping his fingers impatiently.

It was a single piece of elegant lady's stationery, folded and sealed with his name on the outside. On the inside was a single line.

*Please take care of my dogs.*

That was as clear a message as she needed to send. She had run off with Clement again and did not intend to be back. But how had he got a message through to her? Michael had been watching the post and Liv had not been out of the house since their trip to Vauxhall. He signalled to the maid again. 'Take me to her bedroom. We must search for clues to her whereabouts.'

It took less than a minute to find the bundle under the pillow on the bed. He unfolded the scrap of the mail coach schedule, wrapped around a silver brooch formed in the shape of a rabbit. He scanned down the list of stops on the schedule until he came to the Silver Hare.

The packet was small enough to be pitched unnoticed over the fence or slipped into a basket of groceries and had she bothered to separate the two items he'd not have made the connection between them. All in all, it was a clever way to get her to where she needed to be.

He dropped the clues into his pocket and ran for the stairs, calling for the same fast horse that he had taken north the last time he had caught her. Then he set out for Scotland.

The inn he was heading for was two stops further than they had made it thus far, and an overnight stay was inevitable. But it was not too late to keep her from sacrificing her virtue to bind Clement to her, once and for all. He would ride out and save her...

He flinched. His thoughts had drifted to what might happen afterwards. Would there be another night of lying next to her, just out of reach as his body hardened and hers shuddered on the brink of climax? Perhaps, for the return trip, he could procure a private carriage where they might be alone for hours and hours.

He had told her that there was no future in what they had. If he meant to get her back home safely, he had best stop thinking about illicit liaisons. He must not put his wants and desires above those of his employer.

But what if the desires of his employer were not in the best interests of Olivia Bethune? If she was correct and Scofield was trying to kill him, it would not be right to leave the woman he...

He stopped himself and took a deep breath to clear his head and block the words he had been about to think. He was very fond of Liv, nothing more. All the same, he did not want to leave her in the care of a murderer, just because the man was paying him to keep her at home. First, he would get her away from Clement. Then he would find a new, safer place for her to live.

That decided, he spurred his horse in pursuit.

It was much easier to get away from her brother when she did not have Alister helping her and it amazed her that she had not tried it before. She waited until five in the morning, when the night guard was ending his shift. Then she put on her simplest gown and went down the back stairs to the kitchen. She made an excuse to the scullery maid who was building up the fire, telling her that she was going to see if Cleo was whelping.

Then she borrowed a maid's cloak from the pegs by

the door and grabbed a basket from the table. In this simple disguise, she walked through the unguarded gate like a maid on her way to the greengrocer.

As she passed out onto the street she felt a thrill of freedom that she had not felt on previous elopements. No matter what happened later today, she had finally done something for herself. It made her happy in a way that each successive escape with Alister had not.

What did it mean when one was happier alone than with the man one intended to marry? It seemed that she should have sent Alister away some time ago. Just as Michael had said, her feelings for the man she thought she loved were nothing more than habit.

What she felt for Michael Solomon was something quite different. Now that she was alone, she had choices. She could search out her sister and ask for protection. Or she could continue on her journey, confident in the fact that Michael would come to bring her home. But there was no choice really. She would be catching the mail coach as planned. Even if she was dragged back and locked in her room for the rest of her life, she would have a few precious hours unchaperoned with Michael and that was worth any risk.

She walked through London until her feet ached and she had reached the Swan with Two Necks, then bought passage north. She made sure to lower her hood and smile at the ticket seller. If Michael was not able to find the clues she had left for him, she would be remembered here and he could pick up the trail and follow the coach road.

* * *

The ride to the Silver Hare took almost a full day, and she was more than a little tired when the inn came in sight. It was well past supper and she had eaten little more than a bun she had purchased before setting out. Her stomach was growling and her body was weary with the jolting of a coach that was not nearly as well sprung as the Scofield barouche.

When the coach pulled to a stop in the yard, she hopped out and signalled to the driver that she was going no further. She had no luggage to ask for, other than the empty basket she had taken from the kitchen. It would have been nice to have packed a bit of bread and cheese, but she had been too excited to eat and had not thought it necessary.

She entered the tap room and looked around her, tired and confused.

'Lady Olivia Bethune?' The innkeeper stepped forward to greet her.

'Yes,' she said softly, surprised that the man knew who she was.

'You are expected,' he said with a nod and a smile. 'There is a private dining room reserved for you, and a room upstairs, if you would rather go straight to bed.'

'Dinner would be lovely,' she said, praying that these courtesies had been arranged by the man she expected.

'The gentleman is waiting for you in the dining room,' the man supplied, gesturing towards a door at the back of the room.

'Of course,' she said, and allowed him to lead her.

When she arrived at the dining room he was standing with his back to the door, warming his hands by the fire. He did not need to turn for her to know who it was. She could feel the rush in her blood at the sight of him, his broad shoulders and narrow waist, and the golden blond hair that she had imagined in candlelight on the first day she'd seen him, napping in the garden.

But, even beyond that, there was the same inappropriate tugging feeling in her heart, as if she belonged standing at his side and not observing him from a distance. It was unwise to feel such things when she was not sure that he could feel them in return, but she could not seem to help herself.

'What are you doing here?' she said once they were alone, trying to sound impatient rather than relieved.

'I am doing what you want me to,' he said, turning to face her. 'I have come to take you home.'

'What have you done with Alister?' she said, wishing that her voice sounded more convincing.

'I did not do anything to him,' he said with a smile. 'According to the guard I set on him the last time you eloped, he is still in his rooms on Jermyn Street.'

'You are watching Alister?' she said, shocked.

'It is easier to predict these outings when the one who organises them is under observation,' he replied. 'But he did not plan this particular trip, did he?'

She shook her head.

'Where did you get the rabbit brooch?' he asked. 'It was a very clever touch.'

'From my sister's jewellery case,' she said, smiling. 'I wanted to choose something that Molly would not immediately recognise.'

'Well done,' he said with a nod. 'And of course, since it is too late to return home, I have had to reserve a room for you.'

*For us*, she thought urgently.

'What were your plans, upon taking this trip?' he said, folding his arms in front of him like a stern school-master in front of a wayward student.

She thought for a moment and was surprised by the answer that was now clear in her mind. 'At first, it was to have you chase me. You said there would be no more conversations between us, and that I should treat you like I had all the other guards and ignore you. But I do not feel the same way about you that I did the other guards. I could not ignore you, even if I tried.'

His expression softened. And then he said, puzzled, 'At first?'

'The further I got from home, the more sure I became that leaving was the right thing to do. The memories there...' She closed her eyes and took a breath. 'I have nightmares about Father, and sometimes, thinking of Hugh, I get so frightened that I can hardly breathe.'

'In time, it will grow easier,' he said, sounding sympathetic.

'That is what the doctor said, the first time I complained of the problem. He gave me laudanum, but it makes the dreams worse, not better.'

'It has been two years,' Michael reminded her.

'Don't you think I know that?' she snapped, then remembered that it was not his fault if he could not understand. 'Today, as I was leaving, I felt different. Better. Free. And I think, married or not, it is for the best that I leave my brother's house. If I am ever to escape the memories of what happened, I cannot be there any longer, hearing my brother's voice and imagining what he must have done.'

'Running away was still a very dangerous thing for you to do,' he said.

'I was in a mail coach on a main road,' she said, smiling back at him. 'It was not hard to get the ticket. And our previous trip taught me much about the etiquette of travelling in public transportation.'

'I am not talking about the trip,' he said. 'You took nothing but the clothes on your back. You made no plans beyond getting to this inn. And I am sure you do not have enough money to live for more than a day or two. Worst of all, now that you are here, you are alone with me.'

She shivered at the tone of his voice, a delicious tremor that reached all the way to her toes. 'I knew you would find me if I ran away. And you would take care of me, just as you have done since the first day.'

'But this time we are alone together and it is night. Whether you go home or not, I don't think your reputation is likely to survive this trip.'

'No matter what I do, I cannot possibly blot the family escutcheon as badly as my brother has.'

'But a potential husband will not see it that way,' he reminded her.

'There will be no more of those for me,' she said, surprised at how freeing it felt. 'I will not have one chosen by my brother, and I do not mean to search for another on my own. I think Alister has taught me that love and marriage are two different things. I would much prefer the first to the second.' Then she stared at him and smiled, hoping that he could see the feeling in her eyes so she would not have to embarrass herself by declaring something he might not be ready to hear.

He shook his head. 'That only shows how little you know about what goes on between men and women. You might think it possible for a man to give you this love that you imagine. We do not give. We take.'

'There is only one way to settle this argument,' she said.

'And what is that?' he asked, sounding suspicious.

'Through experience. I am going to the room you have reserved for me. I will leave the door unlocked for you, to enter if and when you choose. There, we will debate the merits of love and marriage and see if we can come to an agreement.' Then she turned and walked out of the room.

*Damn.* Even as he had got the room he had been considering the possibility that they might share it. But, talking to her, he had grown more and more sure that, tempting though it was, it was a terrible idea. Then she had kept talking. The longer she had talked, the more sense it had made. He would go to her, just as they both wished. Afterwards, she would think she had his love.

Though it would not be entirely true, neither would it be entirely false. She would have whatever he was capable of giving her. In return, he would offer marriage and they would continue the rest of the way to Gretna Green in the morning.

They would be married before her brother could catch them which, with luck, would prevent Scofield from killing him, as he had threatened to. A minimal amount of research had confirmed that the younger Bethune sister was living with her husband, who was still very much alive. It appeared, once his sister had made her escape, the Duke lost interest and did not carry through on his threats.

So they would marry—for her safety, her honour and his own. It was not the reason she might hope for, but the results would be the same. She would be safely out of her brother's house. And he would have her with him each night, which would ease the obsessive desire he felt when he looked at her now.

But tonight they would not think of the future or the past. For a few hours at least, they would live in the present and take advantage of all the pleasures it had to offer.

## Chapter Fourteen

By the time he opened the door to her room, she had stripped to her shift.

He stood in the doorway for a moment, obviously stunned. And then she realised that she was standing with her back to the fire and the light from it made her last garment all but useless at concealing the curves of her body. She raised her hands to hide herself, then remembered that courage was necessary if she wanted to win the night. She stood perfectly still, allowing him to look.

He closed the door slowly behind him and cleared his throat. 'I thought you might need help getting ready for bed.'

She smiled, allowing him the lie. 'I chose a simple gown because I knew I would not have a maid,' she said. 'I did not want to have to sleep in my clothes like the last time.'

'I see,' he said. But apparently he had not seen enough for he continued to stare at her.

She walked towards the bed, trying not to look as terrified as she felt. She should have eaten in the dining room when she'd had the chance. Her stomach was doing nervous flips and her head was spinning, making her knees give out suddenly as she reached the edge of the mattress. She flopped back upon it, staring at the underside of the bed's canopy and waiting to see what would happen next.

She heard him cross the floor to her until he was standing over her, looking down at her with a bemused expression. 'Do you understand what is likely to happen if I stay here tonight?'

She smiled and nodded, trying not to seem too eager. 'My sister explained some of it. She said that if you are in love there is nothing wrong with acting on it.'

His face clouded. 'I wish you were not so sure of your emotions.'

'You do not want me to love you?' she said, surprised.

'I want you to understand that what we are about to do is not something that can be easily forgotten. I have no intention of bedding you and leaving a bastard behind.'

She remembered what he had said about his own childhood and nodded in understanding.

'That means, if we are to be together tonight, tomorrow we will be completing your trip to Gretna Green. When we return to London, you will be living with me, as my wife.'

When she had set out on this journey she had been unsure how she would cajole him into staying with her more than a night. But now, though he was still unwilling to talk of love, he had offered to keep her with him, always. At least, this time, she was sure of her own feelings. She must trust that his would develop in time. She sat up and held her arms out to him. 'That is more than I ever hoped you would say.'

He sank down on the bed next to her and gathered her into his arms, kissing her. She had not realised how it would feel to be held by him after she had removed her gown. It had been exciting to be near him when dressed. But to be practically naked was like being licked by flames.

He released her long enough to run a finger along the neckline of her shift. 'The next time we are together, I will undress you myself.'

'Is that important?' she said, wondering if she had done something wrong.

'Like unwrapping a present on Christmas Day,' he said, smiling. 'But this is nice as well.' Then he kissed her again, sliding his palms over her breasts. Instantly, her skin tightened and her back arched, as if she could not seem to decide whether to be closer to him or to run away.

He chose for her, wrapping an arm around her waist and scooping her into his lap to straddle him. Then he placed her hands on the buttons of his waistcoat, encouraging her to undo them.

He was right. It was like opening a present, something so wonderful that it made one's hands shake to undo the ribbons. She fumbled with the buttons, and her hands trembled at the knot on his cravat. Eventually she was rewarded by the feel of naked flesh under her fingertips. She buried her face in the hollow of his throat, tasting salt and feeling his blood pulsing just below the skin.

He laughed, a sound that was tense but triumphant, then settled her more securely against his lap. She felt the singing tremor of her body answering the nearness of his and ground her hips against him, letting the feeling grow. He let her play for a moment, then steadied her with a kiss. 'Do not rush, my sweet. We have all night.'

But did they? It was hard to imagine a world where they might have as long as they wanted to love each other. It had been years since her life had been her own. Perhaps this night, for the first time in ages, would be different. But what if it was not? 'Make me yours,' she begged, afraid to miss her chance at happiness.

He shrugged out of his coat and waistcoat and pulled his shirt over his head and tossed it aside. Then he grabbed the hem of her shift and removed that as well, leaving her naked and clinging to him. The kiss that followed was a ravishing of mouth and spirit, a claiming as complete as any ceremony of God or man. When it was through, he cradled her in his arms and rose, then tossed her gently to the centre of the bed, staring down at her as he rushed to remove boots and breeches.

She touched her lips, which still tingled where he had kissed her, and he froze, staring at them in hungry fascination. One hand hung on the waistband of his forgotten breeches, which sagged, revealing the curve of a hip and a thatch of golden hair between his legs.

She wanted to gaze at him as he was looking at her, but she lacked the nerve for it. After visits to museums and a few books found on a forgotten shelf of the family library, she had a vague idea of what she was likely to see once he was fully undressed. But she was not sure if it was polite for the lady to stare back. She bit her finger nervously, trying to decide.

He caught his breath and his eyes flicked downward to her breasts.

She trailed her finger down to follow the path of his gaze. Now she was the one to gasp, for her own touches were more exciting than she'd ever imagined they could be. He was looking at her belly now, and she stroked lower, tracing her navel before dipping her thumb inside it. Then, lower, to stroke her own hip and to cup her sex.

Her hand froze for a moment, as the fingers brushed sensitive places she had not even known she had. The feelings were like those on the night they'd lain together, but stronger, more seductive and compelling.

'Go ahead,' he said, staring down at her with a smile she had never seen before. 'Show me what you want.'

What did she want? She was still not sure. But her body seemed to know. Her legs lolled open. Her hand stroked the opening to her body, and her fingers dipped inside, wanting to fill an emptiness she had never known.

He sighed. 'I have never received a sweeter invitation. Do you understand what is to happen between us?' Then he pushed his breeches to the floor, standing gloriously naked before her.

'I think so,' she said, staring. At least, she hoped so. But, with the size of him, what she was imagining didn't seem quite possible.

'This may hurt,' he whispered as he stretched out on the bed beside her. 'But only the first time. And I will try to be gen—'

She smothered the last word with a kiss. Whatever he was planning could not possibly hurt as much as waiting for it. Her body was slick and she spread her legs wide, then reached for him, dizzy with the feel of his flesh and all the places she wanted to explore.

His sighs turned to groans and for a moment she wondered if it might hurt him as much as it could her. Then he reached for her, pulling her to lie on top of him. The feeling of skin against skin was another unexpected delight, as was the way the sensations changed depending on how she moved.

He groaned again, then laughed. 'You are the devil, woman. I do not know how much longer I can stand to have you wiggling against me without taking action.'

'Do it, then,' she said, feeling incredibly daring. 'Make me yours.'

He slipped a hand between her legs, stroking where

she had stroked, then he thrust a finger into the depths of her body.

She tightened on it, squeezing his hips between her thighs.

He was thrusting into her in a languid rhythm, smiling up at her in the firelight. 'You have been mine in spirit since the first moment we met.'

'And you have been mine,' she said, smiling down at him.

Instead of correcting her, he flicked a finger against the sweetest spot and she thought she might die from the pleasure of it. 'Now we will join, body and soul.'

He put her hand on his member, and together they brought it home to her body. He had been right. At first there was an almost unbearable tightness. Then it eased and the pleasure returned, growing with each subtle movement. Something was building in her, something wonderful. Something she had tasted before when he had looked into her eyes.

And then it happened. She was caught in a whirlwind, unable to control her body or her mind. She cried out, shuddering against him, holding him as if she was afraid he might escape and take this wonder away.

He was shuddering as well, lost in the moment. And then she felt a rush, a final surge of passion, and they collapsed into each other, exhausted.

'I love you,' she said, kissing him on the ear.

He tensed. 'I hope this means you are still willing to marry me.'

It was not the response she expected, but it made her happy all the same. 'Of course. And I shall do my best to be a good wife to you.' Then she remembered Alister and his many prohibitions. 'And in exchange you might do something for me.'

He kissed her back. 'Whatever it is, it is yours.'

'I would like to see my sister again, if only to know she is all right.'

'That is all?' He laughed. 'For a moment I thought you might wish to be draped in Burma rubies, or some equally unattainable...' He stopped, then began again. 'Of course you will see your sister. She is family, after all, and cannot possibly be as difficult as your brother.'

'I love you,' she said again, happiness swelling inside her until she could hardly breathe.

'And we shall be married by this time tomorrow,' he said, tightening his arms about her. 'Let us use the time we have left for some industrious sinning.' And he kissed her with such force that she quite forgot what it was in his words that bothered her.

## Chapter Fifteen

The morning sun rose bright and she could not remember such a beautiful dawn. Light streamed into the window of the inn and over the sheet that covered them both, making it seem such a pure and blinding white that Liv had to shield her eyes when looking at it.

And, best of all, she had slept deeply, free of nightmares. As she sat up, the muscular arm of her lover pulled her back down and into a musky kiss.

'It is morning,' she said, laughing and trying to sit up again.

He groaned into her neck. 'And what does that mean to us?'

She sat up again and bounced on the mattress, making the ropes squeak. 'You promised to take me to Scotland today.'

'I did,' he said with a smile, swinging his legs out of bed and walking to the basin to splash cold water on his face. 'As always, I wait on my lady's every wish.' He was pulling on shirt and breeches. 'I will go downstairs and make arrangements to get us two seats on the next coach.'

'And some breakfast,' she said, smiling back. He had said nothing about love, but at least he was still firmly set on the idea of marriage. It worried her that she knew very little of what life with him might be like. But he had already promised to take her dogs and had nothing against visiting Peg. No matter what else might happen, it would be better than living with Alister.

A few minutes later she had washed and dressed and come down the stairs, scanning the tap room for him, ready for their next great adventure. Instead, she saw the last person she had hoped to see.

'Hugh!' Her smile disappeared and she felt a rising tide of panic, so similar to the way she'd felt when she'd found her father, and when she'd had to admit that her sister had run away.

'Olivia.' Just as he'd been on those other occasions, her brother's face was impassive, but she could feel the rage roiling, just below the surface.

'What are you doing here?' she said, trying to pretend that she did not know what the answer would be.

'I have come to bring you home,' he said, opening his hand to reveal the silver rabbit brooch.

'Surely that was not necessary,' she said, forcing the smile back in place and trying to be glib. 'Mr Solomon has come to fetch me.'

'I am aware of that,' he said. 'He set out after you

yesterday.' There was the faintest emphasis on the last word to remind her that the timeline had too many hours unaccounted for.

'It was already dark when I arrived at the inn,' she reminded him. 'I needed some rest before setting out again, so Mr Solomon was going to make arrangements for this morning.' But she must hope that her brother did not see the tickets he had purchased, for they were going in the wrong direction.

'I see,' Hugh said, staring through her as if he could, indeed, see everything, especially those things she most wanted to hide.

'He has finally convinced me of the error of my ways.' She waved a hand around her to indicate the absence of other men. 'I promise, after this, there will be no more talk of running away with Alister.'

'Solomon convinced you?' Her brother stared at her all the harder. 'And how did he do that?'

She had to come up with a better answer than the truth, or Michael would end up as dead as Richard Sterling was. 'He has been allowing me to get as far as I have on these elopements to prove to me that Alister is not the man I thought he was. When we were together, Alister treated me horribly.'

'In what way?' he said, seeming to grow larger with each word.

'He…' She struggled to find an answer that would not simply turn her brother's anger against Alister who, though not the man she had thought, was also not some sort of villain who deserved punishment. 'He said that after we were married I could not visit Peg.'

'Really?' Hugh replied with a contemptuous raise of an eyebrow.

'And he has not even managed to get to this inn to meet me,' she added. 'I no longer believe he will ever manage to take me to Scotland. And he does not like my dogs,' she added, hoping that this would be enough to convince him.

'And that is all?' he said, clearly suspecting that it was not.

'Of course,' she said quickly. 'He never laid a hand on me, if that is what you are expecting. I just do not like him any more. And I promise you will have no more trouble from me, if we can just return to London and never speak of this again.'

Before he could answer, Michael appeared in the doorway of the tap room, smiling far too broadly for a man who had done nothing more important than settling the bill with the innkeeper.

'L-Lady Olivia.' There was a strange stutter in his greeting, as if he had been about to greet her as Liv, before seeing her brother and remembering the proper form of address.

'Mr Solomon,' she said, carefully putting distance between them. 'My brother has come to escort us home.'

'Home,' he said, in a tone that all but gave away the plans they had made last night.

'Back to London,' she said, willing him to understand the value of discretion.

'Where else would she be going?' Hugh was staring at him with the same penetrating gaze, as if daring him to answer with the suspected truth of what had been going on.

Michael's smile disappeared and he squared his shoulders as if ready to defend her with fists if needed. 'Yesterday evening Lady Olivia made it quite clear that she did not want to return home. She is not happy there. And, for obvious reasons, she does not feel safe. I thwarted her elopement, as you hired me to do. But I will not be party to sending her back to a place she does not wish to be.'

It was exactly the sort of thing she would have hoped her lover would say, given the opportunity. But what she wanted, more than a show of bravery, was some assurance that Michael would live to escape with her some other day.

It was clear from the postures of the two men in the room that what she might want right now did not matter. They were staring at each other, each glare a threat. The tension between them crackled through the air like lightning.

'That is not your decision to make,' her brother said in a soft and dangerous voice. 'Nor is it hers. I am her guardian and I decide where she will live.'

'All the same, I will not move from this spot until I hear from her own lips that she wants to go back to

London,' Michael said, folding his arms and blocking the doorway.

'Do not be ridiculous, Mr Solomon,' she said with a forced laugh. 'Of course I want to go home. Where else would I go?'

'Where indeed?' her brother said, staring at Michael as if he expected an answer.

'I have no idea,' Michael replied, his jaw tightening. 'But as long as she is sure, I will go and see about transport.'

'That will not be necessary,' Hugh said with a smile. 'She will return with me in the Scofield equipage. You may return by whatever method brought you here. And...' his smile widened into a self-satisfied smirk '...since she assures me that her time running off with Clement is officially at an end, I will no longer be needing your services. When you return to London, I will have my solicitor settle with you. Thank you for your time.' The look he gave Michael was the same cold glare he used whenever he chose to dismiss someone from his presence. It was a look that sent even the strongest of men scurrying for the door.

But Michael only stared back at him, ready for the challenge.

Something must be done to end this before she had another dead lover to answer for. 'Thank you for your help, Mr Solomon. It was a pleasure knowing you.'

He turned to her now, as if noticing that she was in the room for the first time. 'Thank you, Lady Olivia.'

His expression was as distant as her brother's and even more convincing. There was none of the warmth that there had been on the previous evening, or any of the days before that. There was only the blank expression of a man who knew his place and would not presume above his station. Then he turned and walked away.

She could not let him go thinking that it was over between them. Despite what her brother had said, she had no intention of giving him up so easily. She made a hasty excuse to Hugh about needing to see to the packing of the luggage she had not brought, then slipped out of a side door to find Michael holding the reins of a hired horse, ready to mount and ride out.

'Michael,' she said, hurrying up to him before he could set off.

'Lady Olivia,' he said with a subservient bow that was a mockery of all they had done in the weeks together.

'I could not let you go without saying goodbye.'

'I believe you did so just now, in the tap room,' he said, turning his attention back to the horse.

'That was for my brother's benefit,' she said, smiling at him, then glancing over her shoulder to make sure that they were not being observed from the windows.

'Your brother,' he said with a shake of his head.

'I could not let him think that anything had happened between us,' she reminded him. 'I am sure he suspects, and you are in enough danger as it is.'

'And so you conveniently denied me, just as you

have done with Clement for two years,' Michael said, unsmiling.

'That is not the same at all,' she argued.

'Of course not. Clement was at least allowed the privilege of offering for you. I am not even worth that.'

'Hugh will say no,' she said, annoyed at his stubbornness.

'Then let us forego the refusal. Run away with me now,' he said, his expression softening. 'We will be able to travel faster on horseback than by carriage and will be in Gretna in no time.'

'He will find us there, and bring me home alone,' she said with a shudder. 'You should know by now what he is capable of.'

'I really have no idea,' Michael said, smiling at her. 'But I know he has done nothing to me so far.'

'Not for want of trying,' she insisted. 'First the horse in Bond Street...'

'We have no proof that it was anything more than an accident,' he insisted.

'The very next day he upbraided me for being with you there. He all but admitted that he had seen us.'

'A coincidence. Nothing more.'

'And what about the thief that set upon you after he saw us at Vauxhall?'

'I was in an area known for footpads,' he said with a shrug. 'I have no reason to suspect your brother of any of this.'

'You do not know him as I do,' she insisted.

'I know that your sister married without incident,' he replied.

'She had to run for her life. And she has made no effort to return to the house since. I have no idea if she is well or ill, or if she is staying away specifically to keep her husband safe from Hugh.'

'All the more reason to leave now,' he said, reaching for her hand. 'You admitted last night what being in his house does to your nerves. You can be free of the nightmares if you run away with me now. I can deal with his threats to my person once you are away from home and I know you are safe.'

She glanced back at the window of the inn and saw a shadow behind the curtain. She pulled away in case it was her brother, embarrassed to discover that it was only a maid. When she turned back to look for it, Michael's hand was at his side again.

'Perhaps it is nothing more than that you are ashamed to be seen with me,' he said with a sad smile.

'It is nothing like that,' she said, thinking of Richard Sterling, and of her father, slumped over his desk and the blood soaking the carpet. 'After what we did last night, I cannot lose you.'

'And yet you have,' he said, shaking his head. Then he mounted his horse and rode away.

He had been a fool. And over a woman who he should have known from the first would never care for him. He had been so careful in the past not to let himself believe lies and open himself to what might happen if one gave way to tender emotions when in the arms of a beautiful woman. Pleasure had always been more than enough to justify the act. But last night he had fallen asleep thinking of a future that meant nothing to her.

She wanted nothing more than to escape her brother. When Clement had failed, she had settled on him. If he had not failed, he'd have shackled himself to her for life. But he had, and she had left him almost as quickly as she had succumbed to him.

So he had gone to the stables immediately after being dismissed by Scofield and hired the biggest brute of a horse they had. Perhaps a stallion that might throw him and knock sense into him if it did not kill him outright.

Then she had come to him again, tempting him. There had been room on the horse for two, if she'd been willing. But she had proved to be just as hesitant and faithless as he'd thought. Even if he'd been able to persuade her to Scotland, she'd have spent the rest of her life looking over her shoulder for her brother and not into his eyes. Now that he'd allowed himself to admit that he wanted a woman to love him as she claimed she did, it had been impossible to settle for less.

He galloped towards London, making sure to leave well ahead of the Scofield carriage so there would be no chance that he might embarrass himself by meeting them on the road. If he was lucky, he would never see either of them again and could pretend that this whole unfortunate incident had never happened.

Of course, the activities of the previous night would be hard to forget. He had been with more than his share of women but had never had a more affecting night than the one he had shared with Liv. After the way she had responded at Vauxhall, he had been more than eager to offer for her, hoping for a lifetime of passion. The desire for coupling had clouded his mind. It had not been love, because there was no such thing.

Of course, whatever the feeling had been was new to him and left him hoping that it would stay for the rest of his life. Even now, he could see the look in her eyes as she had climaxed, one of delighted surprise, and a smile that had been just for him, a thank-you for the gift of satisfaction.

And then she had turned her back on him the first chance she'd got. She had claimed it was fear for him that caused her sudden change of heart. If so, it insulted him that she did not think he could protect himself or her. It was no surprise that, when the first problem arose, she cast him aside, just as she had Clement.

He spurred the horse, trying to get another ounce of speed from him. The quicker he was home, the better. And the sooner he would remember what he had always known: that he was better off alone.

There was no sign of Michael in the coach yard as Hugh helped her into the big black carriage with the Scofield crest on the door. It was probably just as well.

If she had seen him again, she was not sure that she could have helped bursting into tears.

For his safety, it would not do to display too much emotion over her parting from him. It would be better if Hugh forgot all about him by the time they got back to London. Of course, that meant that her life would return to one of confinement and solitude, with not even Michael for company.

Perhaps she could find a way to contact him. His mother had said the house was on Gracechurch Street. Was that enough of a direction to deliver a letter? If she tried to send it, would it be possible to get it past Hugh and whatever new guard he might hire to watch her?

She swallowed another tear, reminding herself that, at the very least, she now had memories to sustain her.

'Did you lie with him?'

Now she was choking on those tears, almost too shocked to speak. 'I beg your pardon?'

'You spent the night alone with Solomon. Did you attempt to win his cooperation by offering him favours?' Her brother was staring at her dispassionately, as if he had not just said the most shocking thing she had ever heard. She supposed it was better than his usual jealousy, but not much.

'I cannot believe that you would suggest such a thing,' she said, turning her face to the window so he could not see her blush.

'That answers my question,' he said, still unemotional. 'It was foolish on your part. If he allowed me to take you away, and he accepts the exorbitant amount of money I pay him, he will not come back to rescue you again. You have gained nothing.'

'I have gained his safety, I hope,' she said, staring back at him defiantly. 'If I promise that I will not see him again, I would hope that you will not track him down and defend my honour over whatever lurid scenarios you are imagining.'

He gave a short bark of mirthless laughter. 'I have no intention of defending your honour if you will not.'

'Then he is safe, as long as I stay away from him?' she said, wondering if she could trust a man who killed with impunity.

'His safety is totally up to you,' he said, reaching into his pocket for a newspaper, signalling that the conversation was at an end.

'And what of Alister?' she said.

'What of him?' he said, not bothering to look up.

'Is he safe?'

Hugh put the paper down, disgusted by the interruption. 'If something was going to happen to Alister Clement, it would have happened long ago. But that does not mean I will allow you to marry him. He is a mealy-mouthed weasel, and always has been.'

'I agree,' she said. 'But I still would not want to see him hurt.'

'You agree?' Newspaper forgotten, Hugh was staring at her in surprise. 'I thought you were lying to me back at the inn, to distract me from Solomon.'

'You were right all along. He was never the right man for me, and I would not have been happy if I had married him.'

'Then I should have paid Mr Solomon far more than I did,' he said with an incredulous expression. 'The man was a bounder who abandoned you after he got what he wanted. But at least he has convinced you to cry off Clement.'

'He did not abandon me,' she said, then added, 'because nothing happened.' Announcing that she had abandoned him for his own good would not make the situation any better with Hugh. And, above all, she wanted Michael to be forgotten and unharmed. 'I have no intention of seeing him again. Why would I?'

'Because you probably think you are in love with him, just as you thought you were with Clement,' her brother said with surprising astuteness.

'That would be very foolish of me,' she said, pretending to agree.

'You are young, and impetuous,' he said, continuing to lecture. 'I hope you will not get into the habit of letting your emotions drive you into situations that are not good for you or the men around you. It is why I keep you cloistered. I cannot trust you not to make things worse for everyone.'

Now he was making it sound as if everything that had happened was her fault for being unreasonable. She bit her tongue, resisting the urge to argue, for it would not help her case.

'Some people are not meant to marry,' he said, giving her a significant look.

'Like you, for example?' she said and watched him flinch.

'Like me,' he said, drawing a breath that made the admission sound more difficult than it needed to be. 'And you as well. Once you are reconciled to the fact, life will be easier for both of us. If you agree not to run away, then I will not need to hire guards to keep you.'

'Then I promise not to run away,' she said, wondering if that was all that was needed to settle the matter.

He laughed. 'On the day when you truly mean that we will finally have an understanding. In the meantime, we shall go home and things will go back to normal, but without the help of Michael Solomon. From now on, I shall watch you myself.'

## *Chapter Sixteen*

Back in London, Michael sat in his empty house, lethargically planning his next move. Another job would be necessary, eventually. But the need was not urgent. When Scofield had paid him off, he had been more than generous.

Too generous, in fact. The size of the settlement hinted at knowledge on the Duke's part, and the desire to buy off a man deemed inappropriate for his sister. The idea made Michael want to tear the bill to bits and return to Scofield House to throw it in the Duke's face.

But one could not eat pride, nor was it likely that a little extra money would make any difference to the way Liv felt about him. She wanted someone who would take her away from her brother, whether it be a king or a footman. But it would not be Michael. Not any more.

There was a knock on the door and a short time later the housekeeper announced the arrival of Mr John Solomon.

'Tell him I am not at home,' Michael said, reaching

for the brandy decanter, in no mood to deal with the other problem in his life.

'He will not listen if you do,' said the man, who had apparently taken the liberty of following the servant into the house.

Michael waved her away and then glared at the man standing in the doorway. 'Am I to be allowed no privacy in my own home?'

'I should think I have given you enough privacy by spiriting your mother away,' he said with a satisfied smile.

'I would rather not think about that,' Michael said, giving the man a pointed look. It was annoying to see the origins of his own features as he did so. Though he had not wanted to believe the fellow's claims or trust his mother's memory, the truth was written in flesh and bone right before him.

But that mattered little to him. He had enough on his mind without adding this. 'State your business and then leave,' he said, waiting.

'I have come to force you to acknowledge me. You cannot avoid me for ever, you know,' Solomon said, smiling his smug smile that was oddly familiar from looking at his own reflection.

'I do not see why not,' Michael replied. 'You have managed to avoid me for nearly thirty years.'

'Not intentionally, I assure you,' the man said with a laugh, then sobered. 'But I do not suppose that matters to you.'

'It does not,' Michael agreed. 'I have learned to get along well enough without you all this time, and I do not need you now.'

'It is not a matter of need on either of our parts,' Solomon said, walking into the room and sitting in the most comfortable chair by the fire. 'Whether you want it to be true or not, we are of the same blood.'

It was a fact. He could not exactly wish away the man, now that he'd appeared. 'I thought myself a bastard,' he snapped at last. 'For decades, I have thought my mother's stories were nothing more than lies.'

'It does you no credit that you did not believe the woman who gave you life,' he said, suddenly disapproving.

'Because her stories were ridiculous,' Michael snapped in return. 'There was no sign of the man she described to me, and no proof of her marriage. When I enquired into the Solomons, they ran me off the property without a word of explanation.'

'Neither family was happy with our marriage,' he said, shaking his head. 'They thought us both too young, and I was a second son with no real fortune. The story is different now, of course. My older brother died without issue. I went to my family first when I returned to England and was greeted as the prodigal, with rings and robes and a fatted calf.' He sounded as ambivalent about it as Michael was of his own parentage. 'But the long and short of it is that you are indeed a legitimate member of the Solomon family, and sole heir to both the estate I gain from them and anything I have earned myself.'

When Michael did not respond, he added, 'Surely it is better to have me than to think yourself illegitimate.'

'It should be,' Michael said, wondering at his own reaction.

'Do not tell me that you never wondered about the identity of the man who sired you. Just who did you expect to find?'

'I did not know,' he lied. But he had assumed that the man was at least landed gentry. And thus he had assumed that his blood was in some way superior to other men in diminished circumstances. His success was guaranteed if he worked hard and was resourceful.

He had never considered that he might really be a member of the Solomon family, who were both landed and wealthy. At one time, he had looked on them with envy. Now, after years of fending for himself and his mother, the gentry seemed soft, naïve and unenviable.

'If you expected a title, I am sorry to disappoint you,' Solomon said, clearly annoyed.

'No,' Michael said, embarrassed that this man would think he still harboured childhood fantasies that a powerful future might some day come to him without the need for hard work. Of course he must understand labour as well or better than Michael did. His life as a common seaman would have been far from easy.

'I did not intentionally abandon your mother, or you,' Solomon reminded him. 'There was never a day in the

last three decades that I did not think of you or wish
to be with you. And now that I am here I am pleased
by what I have found, and disappointed that I was not
here to advise you, and to claim some part in the man
you have become. You have done me proud, Michael.'

Those were precisely the words he had longed to hear
for most of his life. He had wanted a father to be proud
of him, and to regret having cast him off, unnamed. To
find that he had always been wanted… It was as if a
piece of his heart had been missing, and he had learned
to live with the void. But now that the piece was found,
even though it might fit precisely where it belonged, he
could not work up the nerve to place it there.

'All I am asking is that you join me for a drink or
two, and we talk,' Solomon said gently. 'Do me the
courtesy that you would a stranger. I do not demand
that you love me as a father. But since I will be living
with your mother from this moment forward, it will do
neither of us harm to be better acquainted.'

He was right. No matter what Michael might wish,
the man was not going to disappear again. Should he
want to, Michael would feel obliged, for his mother's
sake, to find the fellow and drag him back. 'A drink,'
he agreed, reaching for the brandy decanter and calling
for the housekeeper to bring a second glass.

## Chapter Seventeen

Now that Michael was gone, things were even worse than they had been before his arrival. Liv was bored, frustrated and heart-achingly lonely. She was still trapped in her brother's house, and the nightmares were worse than ever.

She had hoped that, despite what he had said when they'd parted, Michael would relent and come back for her, planning a brave rescue, as Alister had. But there had been no word from him in over a week.

And what was she to do about Alister? She had promised her brother that she would not be running away with him again, but she was not sure that Alister knew or agreed. He had been as plain in his break from her as Michael had been, but he had since smuggled several messages to her, which she had burned without reading. It did not matter to her if he meant to apologise or wished another trip to Scotland. It was over between them.

She wondered if he would be waiting on the next

day's visit to Mrs Wilson, ready to eat his words and disavow the way he had rejected her in the inn. If he did, it was proof that he had not understood any better than she had, that time could not be turned back to play out in the way one wanted it to.

But that did not mean one could not try to change the future. Her breath caught in her throat. She had not been truly happy until she had decided to take matters into her own hands and escape the house. And now she'd forgotten and gone back to being passively unhappy. She needed to take control of her future or she would spend the rest of her life staring out of the window.

First, she waited until Hugh was out of the house and made a trip to his office, searching the desk until she found the information that she needed. The next day, as the footman loaded the charity baskets into the carriage, she requested one extra and prepared the contents herself. Then she hurried Molly to the carriage and dragged her through the stops until they arrived at Mrs Wilson's house.

'The Duke says I am not to let you go in alone,' the maid said, clearly afraid that she was about to anger either her mistress or her employer.

'It is all right,' Liv said, giving her an encouraging smile. 'In fact, it might be easier if you come in with me this time.'

She let Molly lead the way up the stairs, carrying the basket herself. The door opened before the girl could manage to knock.

'I have waited so long. Why did you not answer my messages?' Then Molly was pulled, squealing, into the room and kissed on the lips before Alister had even realised that he'd grabbed the wrong woman. He thrust her away again almost as quickly, wiping his mouth and cursing.

'I did not answer because I did not want to run away again,' Liv said in a calm voice, staring at the man in front of her. He was a handsome enough man under normal circumstances. But as he was now, his face red with anger and embarrassment over a trifling incident, she wondered what it was that she had ever been attracted to.

'Do not be ridiculous,' he said. 'You have been trying to get out of your brother's house since the first moment we met.'

'I have changed,' she said, handing the basket to Mrs Wilson. 'If I ever manage to leave Hugh's home, it will not be to marry you.' She turned, preparing to go again.

'You cannot leave me,' Alister said, grabbing her arm, his anger replaced by amazement.

'On the contrary. You were the one who left me. I think you were quite adamant about it when we were last together.'

'That was said in the heat of the moment,' he said. 'You cannot hold me to it.'

'Hold you to your words?' she said, surprised. 'I thought it was the hallmark of gentlemen not to say things they do not mean.'

'When one is in love, it is different,' he said.

'But do you love me, really?' she asked. 'And did I ever love you? Or were we both simply in love with the idea of being together?'

'Of course we are in love,' he said, dismissing her words, as he had done so many times recently. Then he reached to pull her to him in an embrace that he probably thought would make all things right again.

She stepped clear of his outstretched arms. 'Well, I am no longer sure of my feelings.' It was a white lie, for she grew more sure of what she felt each moment she spent with him. 'And thus, I must release you from any promises you have made me.'

'I do not want to be released,' he said with a huff. 'I want you to come to your senses.'

She shook her head sadly. 'That is the trouble, Alister. I think I have.'

'You must realise that, after the things we have done together, your reputation is ruined. No man would ever want you after what we have done.'

Blackmail. It should not have surprised her, but it did. 'Those words are all I need to be sure my instincts are correct,' she said with a sad smile. 'It does not matter if no other man wants me, Alister. I have no intention of marrying you just because you are my last hope. I am sorry, but I simply cannot.'

Then she stepped out into the hall, dragging Molly after her, and shut the door. They hurried down the steps in silence and made it all the way to the coach before Molly blurted, 'What am I to tell the Duke?'

Liv rolled her eyes. 'About this stop? Anything you like. Tell him the truth. I think he will approve of what I have done. But about the next stop?' She smiled. 'If you value your position, you will not say a word.' Then she gathered the last basket close to her heart and signalled the driver to take them to Gracechurch Street.

Michael was in the sitting room staring into the fire when he heard a knock at the door. A short time later, the housekeeper showed his father into the room. Without waiting for an invitation, John Solomon took the chair opposite him, then glanced at the brandy bottle.

From another man, it might have been a hint that a drink was requested, but today Michael sensed disappointment in the look, as if the man did not like to see him drinking spirits so early in the day.

Michael drained the glass he was holding, filled it again with a slow deliberate motion, then put it down. 'What is it now?'

John Solomon smiled with equal deliberation, as if to say he was not likely to be put off by a frown and harsh treatment. 'Does a father need a reason to visit his son?'

Michael sighed, reminding himself that, now that he was beginning to know his father, he had vowed to be less of a thorn in the man's side. 'I suppose not. But that does not keep me from wondering.'

Solomon pulled a sheaf of papers from his pocket

and set them on the table between them. 'A few pages need your signature, if we are to finalise the details of your annuity.'

'I have told you before, this is not necessary,' he reminded the man. All the same, he took the papers, scanning the pages and raising his eyebrows at the amount described.

'Of course not. But that does not mean you might not want it in the future.' Solomon shrugged. 'I simply want to give you the freedom to do whatever you want. If you do not need the money, put it in trust for my grandchildren.'

'You will have no grandchildren because I never plan to marry,' he said. Then he remembered that there was a chance that he might be less than nine months from fatherhood. He had promised that he would not leave a bastard behind. But in a moment's anger he might have done just that.

Solomon tapped his knee and nodded. 'You cannot know what will occur in the future. When you meet the right woman and fall in love…'

Michael laughed. 'I have no intention of falling in love with anyone.'

'Your mother has told me of your peculiar aversion to it.' Solomon smiled. 'She says you are independent to the point of stubbornness and solitary long after a man should be settling down. She says that you insist you will not marry, since you have no faith in the emotions behind such bonds.'

'Love is nothing more than a fairy story told to children,' he said, knowing that this was a weak excuse to explain what he felt.

'Because your mother told you of it?' he said, arching an eyebrow.

'She...' He stopped. She had told him of the enduring power of true love. And it appeared that in her case it was true.

Solomon ignored his pause. 'As I said before, if you do decide to marry, surely it will be better to have a name and family to impress the family of your betrothed,' the man said in a coaxing tone. 'The Solomons are not the best family in England, but neither is there anything particularly objectionable about them. With the addition of my fortune, there are few who would turn up their noses if you wished to make a match.'

'I do not wish to match with anyone. And I certainly do not care what Liv's brother thinks of me,' he announced.

Solomon arched an eyebrow. 'Rejected already, eh?'

'It had not progressed to an offer,' he admitted, wondering why he was confiding in his father. Then he added, 'I do not think the lady's affections were as firmly fixed as...'

*As mine were.*

'As they could have been,' he finished, embarrassed at what he had almost admitted.

'And because this woman broke your heart, you have vowed never to marry. Perhaps you have given up too soon,' Solomon replied. 'Present yourself to the girl again. Inform her of your change in circumstances and see if it makes a difference.'

'If it did, it would only prove to me that she could not love me for myself,' Michael said, embarrassed that he would share such a fear with a man he barely knew.

'She cast you off?' Solomon said with a thoughtful look.

'Not exactly,' Michael said, remembering how it had ended between them. He had not given her a chance to do so. He had been too quick to do the thing himself.

'If you are at fault for the breach, you should do what you can to mend it,' Solomon said. 'If it is love, then all will be right again, just as it is between myself and your mother.'

And that was another thing he did not understand. 'How did you know, when you found her, that my mother would still be waiting for you?'

'For the same reason that I waited,' he said with a fond smile. 'The bond we had was unbreakable. That is what it means to love.'

If that were true, Liv would be waiting for him to come back, and would continue to wait, even though he might never return. And he had been too cowardly to give her any hope. But now he was likely banned from the house, the same way Clement had been.

There was a knock on the door, and the sound of the maid speaking to someone in tones of surprise. Michael pinched the bridge of his nose and reached for the brandy bottle, in no mood to deal with whatever it was that elicited such a response.

'It might be good news,' his father suggested, eyeing the bottle in disapproval.

'Even if it is, it is probably nothing I want to hear,' he replied.

The housekeeper appeared in the doorway to the sitting room holding a wicker hamper that seemed to rock in her arms as if it had a life of its own. She held it out to him. 'The maid who delivered it said you would know who it had come from.'

As she spoke, a small black nose appeared over the top of the wicker, snuffling industriously in his direction as if it were possible to read everything about him from the scent on the air. Then the small canine head that it belonged to was revealed, the bug eyes of Caesar the pug like two black marbles staring at him, his fat front paws hanging over the basket's rim. There was an awkward lunge as the housekeeper struggled to keep control and the little dog half jumped, half spilled onto the floor, scrambling forward to sniff his boot.

He sighed. 'Yes, I know where it came from.' But he was less sure as to why. 'Was there a note of any kind?'

The servant shook her head.

Liv had wanted him to take her dogs if she was unable to care for them. Had she left her brother's house? But why would she give him only one dog? Was this meant as some sort of consolation? Was it an invitation? An apology? Without meaning to, he was attaching all sorts of meaning to the little animal, hoping that it was a sign there might be a future between them, even after what he had said to her.

Perhaps it was just a sign that Cleo had delivered her pups and she had too many dogs and was giving them to whoever she could think of to prevent the footmen from drowning them.

'A gift from the lady we have been discussing?' his father asked.

He nodded. 'But I have no idea what it means.'

Then the dog hunched, opened its mouth and retched up a soggy lump of torn paper.

'It appears she *did* write to you,' his father said, staring down at his feet.

He nodded. Of course the message was now unintelligible. But it was something to know it had been done. 'Caesar has a reputation for being a very bad dog,' he said, staring down at the little fellow. 'Perhaps she would have been better off sending Cleopatra.'

At the mention of his mate, the dog's ears pricked up.

'Who is Cleopatra?' his father asked.

Now, the dog was trotting around the room, sniffing under chairs in search of her, ending with a careful search of his own basket, as if forgetting that he had arrived alone. He looked up at Michael, confused, then raised his head and made a sound that was an ungodly cross between a growl and a screech. He stopped long enough to make another circuit of the room and then howled again, clearly distressed.

His father covered his ears and Michael felt all the hairs on his arms rise as the poor dog let out a third yowl, trailing away into a whine. Then he threw himself dejectedly down on the rug and stared up at Michael as if all the ills of the world rested on his furry shoulders.

Michael smiled. 'Cleo is his lady love.'

'Can dogs have such a thing?' his father asked, surprised.

'They can,' Michael said, smiling. 'Dogs love each other deeply, just as people do.' He laughed, and the feeling was as deep and freeing as seeing the light in Olivia's eyes when they had awakened together at the inn. It was a feeling he had refused to name until today, a feeling that he could no longer deny.

Liv had sent him a message and he did not need a piece of paper to tell him what it was. She loved him, and she was waiting.

## *Chapter Eighteen*

Hugh had finally achieved his goal. He no longer needed a guard to keep her in the house. Since Michael had gone, there was no reason to run away. If he did come for her, she needed to be in the first place he would look.

She had been hoping for something that would be serious enough to make Hugh either summon him or send her away in disgrace. But, two weeks after their night together, her monthlies had come, removing any hope of an unexpected child.

Another unwanted bonnet had arrived from the milliner's, a probable message from Alister about another plan for elopement, as if he thought that the horrible things he had said in Mrs Wilson's flat could be undone with nothing more than time. She had turned it away unopened, hoping that the message was sufficient to make him leave her alone.

The days dragged on, empty of chess games and clever conversation. Breakfasts with her brother passed in miserable silence. If he noticed her unhappiness at all, he chose not to acknowledge it. This morning, he pushed the marmalade in her direction as if it were the solution to all her problems.

'No, thank you,' she said, pushing it back down the table.

'It is your favourite,' he coaxed.

'What is wrong between us cannot be solved by a spoonful of preserves or an extra lump of sugar in my tea,' she replied.

'But you must eat something,' he said in a gruff tone that barely disguised his concern. 'Starving yourself will do nothing to change your circumstances. You are wasting away.'

'If you truly cared about my wellbeing, you would let me go,' she said.

'Go where? With whom? And what would you do when you got there?' he said, obviously frustrated. When she did not answer, he added in a tone that was almost gentle, 'No matter how it seems to you, Liv, I have acted with your best interests at heart.'

'Then please stop helping me,' she said, throwing her napkin aside. 'If I have any more help from you, I swear it will break what is left of my heart.' Then she rose, leaving her breakfast uneaten, and stormed down the hall to the sitting room to begin another empty day.

All men were idiots. Especially men like Michael Solomon. He had not answered her gift, though she was sure the letter that accompanied it had been quite plain.

She had sworn that her words at the inn had been nothing more than lies told to protect him from the wrath of her brother. Though she still loved him as much as ever and still wanted to marry him, she had been afraid of inflaming Hugh's temper by eloping right in front of him. Now that things were calm, it would be even easier to sneak away than it had been on that day.

They could even take the dogs with them. She had added a playful line in her note about the need to reunite Caesar and Cleopatra, telling him that the poor bitch was pining for her mate and begging him to at least show the pugs some sympathy and to visit her in the garden, where they could talk, just as they used to.

It had been over a week. He'd had ample opportunity to return her dog or at least smuggle in an answering note. But he had done nothing. Apparently, the fact that he had not spoken of his love for her on the night they were together had meant exactly what it seemed to. His feelings for her were not as deep as they should have been, and his offer of marriage was made simply to coerce her into bed.

Not that trickery had been necessary. She had been the one to trick him. When Peg had told her of the act of love, she'd been speaking of a man who had been willing to fight to get to her. She'd had no advice to give on what one should do when one had chosen unwisely. Michael Solomon had promised the moon, then taken the money her brother had given him and disappeared.

She stared out through the window of the sitting

room into the garden, at the tree where he should be sitting. Before she had met him, she had never seen the bench as such an empty place. Perhaps if she saw Cleo, she would feel better. A least they could be miserable together.

She went to the kitchen and collected the usual selection of scraps and bones, ignoring the pitying looks of the kitchen staff and the worried encouragement to take some biscuits for herself as well. Then she went through the back door and out to the kennel.

'Cleopatra?' The kennel was empty, and no one answered her calls. Perhaps she was having her puppies. Liv spun around, scanning the grounds, rushing to search under plants and bushes in case the pug was hiding from her. But Cleo was a good dog who never hid. She always came when she was called.

Then she saw her worst fear. The back gate was open. Cleo had been inconsolable since she had sent Caesar to live with Michael, and now she had escaped to find him. She heard a distant bark and tears choked her throat as she rushed out of the yard, searching up and down the street for a flash of tan fur. She'd lost too much in recent days. She had to find the dog.

And then she saw the carriage.

It was parked halfway down the road in the place that always seemed to be chosen when someone wanted to spirit her away from the house, and the door stood open. As she ran towards it, she saw Cleo, a fresh bow upon her collar, hanging from the window. She rushed the last few feet without bothering to see who was inside, reaching for her dog as she took a seat, letting the little animal burrow into her lap and shower her with wet kisses. Then her second dog appeared, popping from a hamper on the seat beside her as if he wished to surprise her.

The door closed and they set off. 'I am happy to see that someone here is being greeted with pleasure.'

Liv turned her head, trying to prevent Cleo from licking the tears from her face as Caesar danced around her feet, tugging at her skirts. Michael was sitting in the seat opposite. 'You took my dog.'

'Just as you wished me to,' he reminded her. 'When you left this house for good, you wanted to know they would be taken care of.'

'Am I really leaving my brother's house?' she said, hardly daring to hope, but noticing that he had not said *we*.

'I came back for you,' he said, then smiled. 'Because I knew you were waiting for me. And because I love you.'

She laughed in surprise. 'You suddenly believe that?'

'Not suddenly,' he admitted. 'I have come to the conclusion slowly, dragged kicking and screaming towards the truth. But I arrived there, all the same. I love you and I am not sure it is possible to live without you.'

For a moment she was not sure she'd heard correctly. But she was afraid to ask him to repeat it, lest it turn out she had heard wrong. She looked out of the window at the streets passing by. 'We are not headed for Gretna. I have started for it often enough to know the best way to go.'

He laughed. 'No, we are not. There are things that must be settled first. I suspect your brother will be hot on our heels and would stop us long before Scotland, should you still wish to go there. It will be easier to get away if we settle things with him now, rather than letting him run us down.'

He meant that she must talk with her brother, she supposed. He had been brave enough to stand up to the Duke weeks ago. She was the one who could not seem to do it. Even now, the thought of a confrontation with him left her feeling light-headed.

'Is there no other way?' she asked.

'It will be easier than you think,' he said. 'You have let him rule your life and dominate your fears for too long. If you wish to get away from him, you will need to make an effort.'

Did she still wish to get away? Of course she did. But how many times in the last weeks had she really believed it was possible? Even halfway to Scotland, it had been easy for him to drag her back because her heart had never really left the cage that had been created for it.

'Where are we going?' she said, looking out of the window at the clean and modest neighbourhoods passing by outside as she felt the carriage drawing to a stop.

'We are here,' he said. It was no real answer, but he

was opening the door and helping her down. If she loved him, she must trust.

Before her feet had touched the ground, her sister Margaret enveloped her in a hug and a shower of tears. 'Liv! I have missed you. I have even missed Caesar. And here is Cleo! You lovely little dog.' She reached down to scoop up the dog that had helped her escape months ago. 'Come inside.' She was leading the party up the short walk to a little house, bouncing the dog in her arms. 'Of course you must remember David.'

'Mr Castell,' Liv said, still breathless with surprise.

Peg beamed a smile over her shoulder. 'And our new friend, Mr Solomon. Thank you so much for returning her to us.'

For a moment, Liv could not seem to manage anything more than a soundless flapping of her jaw, then the tears began to come and she threw herself into her sister's arms once more, crushing the dog between them.

Peg's voice was watery as well. 'When you didn't answer my letters, I was worried that something had happened or that perhaps you did not want to acknowledge me.' She passed the pug to Liv and reached into a pocket for a handkerchief that was already crumpled and wet. 'Curse these tears. I cry so easily now.'

Liv closed a hand on her shoulder and searched out Mr Castell to give him the warning glare of an outraged older sister. 'If there is anything at all wrong, you must let me set it right.'

At this, her little sister laughed through the tears. 'You have not noticed? You are being a goose.' Now, Peg was pulling her into the house, which was small but warm and welcoming. When she withdrew, Liv saw the obvious bulge of her sister's belly and the warm, protective look that her husband cast her as they stepped over the threshold.

'You are *enceinte*?' Liv said, amazed.

'As big as Cleopatra,' Peg said, grinning. 'I swear, missing you is the only unhappiness I have had since I ran away. We travelled all over England before going to Scotland. I have even seen the Continent. I wrote to you nearly every day, but you never answered.'

'Hugh would not let me see the post. He is as awful as ever. And I have been so frightened, being alone in the house with him.'

Peg flushed. 'We have settled in London for the sake of the baby. I wrote to him, hoping that, now we are married, he would let me visit you. But he refused. You are right. He is horrid. And as far as I can see, there is no reason for it.'

Liv shot an outraged glance towards Michael. 'You should not have brought me here. We cannot let Hugh anywhere near the child.'

'Hugh?' Peg said with surprise. 'Why would I...? Wait. You really have received none of my letters. Not even the first one, though Lord knows why he would hide that knowledge from you.'

'Not a word,' Liv assured her.

'Then you do not know.' Peg looked at her husband. 'She does not know.'

'Know what?' Liv said, confused.

'It is not Hugh you have had to fear all this time,' her sister assured her. 'When we left London, David and I discovered much about our brother. The murderer was a woman.'

'A woman,' she said, shocked.

'Someone with ties to Hugh. He entertained a lady in our home on the night Father was murdered. And later he sought to have her committed to a lunatic asylum for her mad and murderous rage.' Peg shuddered. 'I have no idea what she has against our family, other than a twisted desire to do what she thinks is best for Hugh.'

'I think I have seen her,' Liv said, shocked. 'Disguised, of course. I have no idea of her identity, but she is still seeing our brother. We saw her in Vauxhall. And I think she sent me a letter.' Had the ragged printing of the bloody note been a woman's hand? She could not tell.

'She has been lurking outside your house,' Michael said in a warning tone. 'I have seen her on the back walk, staring in the windows.'

'He is still obsessed with a woman he knows he cannot have,' Peg said, considering. 'Does he not know how dangerous it is, for him and for all of us?'

'I doubt he cares,' Liv said. 'Now that you know what love is, would you give up your Mr Castell for the sake of the family?'

'You know I could not,' her sister replied. 'Else I would not have left you alone. But I had no idea that you might still be in danger from this woman.'

'I am not,' she said. 'But Michael is.'

'It was a man who attacked me,' he replied.

'Are you sure?' she said. 'Did you see your attacker clearly either time?'

He hesitated and then countered, 'I am still not sure that both times were not accidental.'

'Perhaps if we appeal to Hugh to control her?' Peg suggested. 'He thought he would keep us both safe by keeping us from society. Or perhaps he simply did not want us to know the truth.'

'I cannot tell what his motives might be,' Liv said. 'But if he is not the murderer...'

'Fairly safe to assume he is not, if he is there to protect you and keeps hiring guards,' Michael said softly. 'It was why I did not rush you to Scotland. You deserve time to decide what is best for you. If you think it is safest to live with Scofield, I will take you back there.'

Liv started, embarrassed that she had forgotten all about the final destination she had been hoping for when he had taken her from the house today.

'Or you can remain here with us,' Peg reminded her. 'I have invited you so many times. You can have a season, if you wish. I doubt Hugh will try to control you, once you are out of the house.'

'But...' She thought he had dragged her back from the inn. But that was not totally true. She had gone willingly, for Michael's sake. There was no proof that he would have used force, had she resisted.

And now her heart was near to bursting at the excitement of possibility. She could go wherever she wanted. But the one place she wanted to see was the one that Michael had barely mentioned.

A stern voice cut through her indecision. 'She will be coming home with me.' Hugh was standing in the doorway, arms folded, the two little dogs staring up at him wide-eyed with shock.

'I am sorry, Your Grace. I do not recall inviting you into my home.' This came from David Castell, who positioned himself between his wife and the Duke.

Hugh gave an imperious wave of his hand. 'I am sure there was something in one of Margaret's letters on the matter.'

'Unless she says otherwise, you will be leaving without Olivia,' Michael said, taking a similar stance to Mr Castell.

'And what gives you the right to an opinion?' Hugh said with a cold laugh.

'I am in love with your sister.'

Liv sucked in her breath, surprised to hear him admit it aloud to someone other than her. It was proper etiquette to approach one's guardian before offering. But then, it was also to be done before a night of passion, so she could forgive herself for being somewhat confused.

'I wish to offer for her,' Michael said, ignoring the smirk on Hugh's face.

'You cannot possibly think I'd entertain the idea that…'

'That you would allow your sister to marry the legitimate heir to the Solomon family of Northumberland,' he completed, stopping Hugh's insult cold on his lips. 'My family fortune is chiefly in mining. But my father is recently returned from India and has made his own money in the sale and trade of precious gems. He went to Cambridge with your father.'

Liv tried not to gasp and failed.

Michael turned to her with a smile. 'Much has happened in the last few weeks. I will tell you all about it, in time.'

Then he turned back to Hugh. 'If it will make you more comfortable, I will cease my employment as an enquiry agent. I have ample funds at my disposal to live off the interest. I can also move to a fashionable neighbourhood where she might be more at home—'

'I would quite like to see your house,' Liv interrupted. 'I have been imagining it for weeks.'

'No!' Hugh's voice cut through their conversation. 'She is not going anywhere but home. And she is not marrying anyone. Even if she was, it certainly would not be you.' He stabbed a finger in Michael's direction.

Liv looked at him, as if for the first time. He was very frightening when he was angry. But she could remember him long before her father had died, when he was a doting older brother and not the strange, cold creature that he had become. If, as Peg said, he was not a murderer at all, then he had much less power over her than she'd thought. 'I will be of age in three months,' she said softly. 'And then I am going to marry Michael, no matter what you might say.'

'You cannot,' Hugh said, as if the command was all that should be necessary.

'I can and will,' she said, her strength growing with each word. 'Since you persist in objecting, I will marry him as soon as we can get to Scotland.'

'I will not allow it,' he announced.

'Perhaps you can stop me if you carry me bodily from the room,' she said, considering.

'And I will not allow that,' Michael replied, taking off his coat, as if preparing to fight. 'Whatever she does, it will be her choice.'

'I will call you out,' Hugh insisted.

'And I will let you shoot me dead in a field,' Michael said with a shake of his head. 'What good will it do you to have one more death attached to your name?'

'That is precisely what I am trying to prevent,' he said, looking wildly around the room.

Liv smiled at him in sympathy. Now that he no longer had the power to frighten her, it was much easier to see a way forward. 'The problems you are imagining have nothing to do with me. They are between you and the woman we saw at Vauxhall, and I refuse to be held prisoner by them any longer.'

She reached out to Michael, twining her arm with his. 'How long will it take to get to Gretna Green?'

He grabbed his coat and laughed. 'I do not know. I have only ever been halfway there.'

'Let us find out.' Then she pushed past her shocked brother, whistled for the dogs and they were on their way.

They rushed together to the carriage that had brought them to her sister's house and he all but tossed her into her seat, slamming the door behind him and signalling the driver with a single tap on the front wall that set them off. Then Michael dropped back into the seat beside her, smiling.

She smiled back at him, happy but confused. 'Now, what was all that fustian you were spouting about being the heir to a fortune?'

'It is God's truth,' he said, shaking his head as if he still found it amazing. 'I owe my mother an apology for a lifetime of doubt about my parentage. But the short of it is, John Solomon has come home and brought a sizeable fortune along with him. He is living on Grosvenor Square with my mother. They were married all along and are just as in love as the day they met. It is quite sickening, really.'

'I think it is romantic,' she said, thinking of the mischievous woman he had introduced as his mother.

'Carrying on, at their age,' he said, shaking his head in disapproval.

She laughed. 'And am I to take it that when you reach their age you will be beyond the pale?'

'That is a different matter entirely,' he said, shocked.

'Of course,' she said with a nod. 'But, beyond your parents' shocking behaviour, you have found that you are not a bastard, after all.'

'A perfectly ordinary, legitimate son,' he said. 'I hope that does not disappoint you.'

'I love you, no matter who you are,' she said, snuggling into his side.

'Then, if you do not mind terribly, I will not give up my job,' he said. 'It is one thing to accept money I have not earned, and quite another to change my entire life because of it. I quite enjoy what I do to make my living and suspect I would not be as happy living the idle life of a gentleman.'

'I think I should find it rather interesting to be the wife of a gentleman detective,' she said staring up at him.

'That is good, because I have been imagining you as such for quite some time,' he said, then cleared his throat as if choking on a hard truth. 'And, given the additional information about my own life and my parents' devotion to each other, I have had to revise certain opinions on human affection that I might have expressed to you earlier.'

'Are you saying you love me?' she asked, slipping a hand inside his coat and wrapping it around his waist.

'No,' he said, surprising her. 'I am trying to apologise for not saying that I loved you ages ago. The truth is, I adore you and I was an idiot to deny the fact.' He reached into his pocket then and produced a ring set with a sapphire of impressive size, took her hand and slipped it on her finger. 'Perhaps it is not the dark blue that most buyers value. But it is the exact colour of your eyes.'

She stared down at the stone, amazed.

'It is a gift from my father, as well as from me. Apparently, I have been denied the benefits of my family for some time. I was dubious of his gifts at first.' He stared down at the ring on her hand. 'But I cannot deny that I enjoy treating you in the manner you deserve.'

'I do not want anything more than to be your love,' she said. 'But the ring is very nice. And it is the only thing I have, since I left the house with nothing.'

'Nothing but your dogs,' he reminded her. 'After we are properly married, we will appeal to your brother for the release of your other possessions. In the meantime, you have but to ask and I can provide for you.'

'Anything?' she said with a smile.

'Anything at all,' he assured her.

'Then I want you to kiss me,' she replied, wrapping her arms about his neck.

'Your wish is my command,' he said, pulling the shades on the carriage windows and settling into her arms.

## Epilogue

Hugh Bethune, Duke of Scofield, stalked to his carriage, signalling the coachman with a single word. 'Drive.'

'Home, Your Grace?'

'No!' What would be the point of that now? 'Somewhere. Anywhere. It does not matter.' He climbed into the body, slumping in his seat, hand over eyes as the vehicle set off into an uncertain future.

God, he felt weak, so tired that he could barely hold himself upright. It was as if he had been coiled like a spring, ratcheted tight for two long years, a slammed door against the inevitable. And now someone had released the tension, picked the locks and he had no energy left in him to fight.

He had failed.

When they had been younger, a simple warning of propriety had been enough to hold both of his sisters in the house. A knitted brow and a frown, along with a firm reminder that they were in mourning was all it had taken to keep them out of society and away from trouble. But as the months had passed and the death of Scofield senior had grown distant, their thoughts had turned to marriage, just as if they were ordinary girls and not the unpredictable creatures he had known them to be.

He had resorted to shouting, then lies, and finally guards, and in the end none of it had mattered. They'd both escaped to marry men who saw nothing but pretty young victims of a dictatorial older brother. They probably thought of themselves as knights rescuing distressed damsels and not further victims of the Scofield curse.

But he had been in the house the night his father had died, just as they had. He knew he'd not killed the old man, though it had been easier for the sake of the family to let the world assume that he had. After repeated questioning, the Runners had assured him that there was but one servant in the house that could not be accounted for at the time of the murder.

When he'd discovered the body of their maid in the garden, he'd told no one. The servant who had helped him carry the body to the river might have guessed the truth, but he had been paid well to keep his mouth shut and was on his way the next morning, just as horrified at the truth as Hugh had been.

He laughed at the memory, scrubbing his face with his hands, as if it were possible to wipe away the fears of what might happen to those two poor, unsuspecting idiots who were now his brothers by marriage. One of them, or perhaps both of them, would soon find out what he had known for years: madness ran in his family, and no one who loved them was safe.

\* \* \* \* \*

*If you enjoyed this story, be sure to read
the first book in Christine Merrill's
Secrets of the Duke's Family miniseries*

Lady Margaret's Mysterious Gentleman

*And whilst you're waiting for the next book,
why not check out her other great reads*

The Brooding Duke of Danforth
"Their Mistletoe Reunion" *in Snowbound Surrender*
Vows to Save Her Reputation

*Look out for the next book in the
Secrets of the Duke's Family miniseries,
coming soon!*